THE ADVENTURES OF
CAPTAIN KITCHEN

SHAWN OETZEL

THE ADVENTURES OF CAPTAIN KITCHEN

by

Shawn Oetzel

2nd Edition 2018
1st Edition Trade Paperback 2013
All Rights Reserved

Dark Recesses Press
657 Craigen Road
Newburgh, Ontario
Canada K0K 2S0

Edited by Melanie Choly
Cover Art © 2013 Marc Nelson

Library & Archives Canada ISBN
978-1-988837-06-2

Also by Shawn Oetzel

The Agency

Dying Moon

ACKNOWLEDGEMENTS

I would first and foremost like to thank Jodi Lee, Melanie Choly and everyone else at (former) Belfire Press who worked on this book in an effort to make it the best it could be. Your time and hard work is greatly appreciated!

Very special thanks go out to artist, educator and director Marc Nelson, who created the cover art. Mr. Nelson you are a highly gifted artist and brought Captain Kitchen to life in a way my words alone could never have done. Thank you my friend!

Thanks to my children for continually understanding the eccentricities of having a writer for a father.

DEDICATION

For the best grandparents anyone could ask for, John and Millie Cagle, who would have found having a writer for a grandson to be pretty cool. I miss you every day.

Table of Contents

CHAPTER 1

The Beginning

Benjamin Winters—Benji to his close friends—paused in applying frosting to a large chocolate cake when he heard the blare of police sirens growing near. Unfortunately it was a sound he, like most of the citizens of Range City, had grown accustomed to in recent months. The once fair city had become a virtual den of villainous activity, with criminals scurrying about like rats, crawling out of every nook and cranny the city had to offer.

He shook his head in frustration, the sirens reaching a crescendo as the police cruisers passed directly in front of the restaurant where he was working. Slowly, the sound began to fade away as the police made their way to the newest in a seemingly never ending list of crime scenes. Only when the wail of the sirens finally dissolved into silence did he turn his attention back to the birthday cake awaiting its final touches.

As head chef of Chez Louis Ristoranté, it was one of his many pleasures to apply the decorative frosting designs to the pastries and desserts the restaurant was known for. This particular cake was for a large party in the banquet room, a city councilman's 50th birthday, and it was to be the highlight of the evening's festivities.

"If they spent as much time trying to figure out a way to stop some of this crime, as they did planning these ridiculous parties, maybe this city would be a bit safer," he mumbled to no one in particular.

As he was putting the final bit of decoration—a large blooming flower—on top of the cake, a young cook named Jimmy Davis burst through the double doors.

"Did you hear all the commotion?" he asked.

1

"Yeah I heard 'em," Benji answered noncommittally. "That's a sound I've heard a lot lately."

"I know watcha mean Cap, but what can ya do?"

Jimmy always called him Cap. It was an annoying habit the young cook had picked up when he found out Benji once held the rank of Captain in the Army Corps of Engineers. The kid did not mean any harm by it, so he let it go without comment. Besides, there were far worse things one could be called.

"Well, right now you can help take this cake out to Councilman William's party," he ordered in his best Captain's voice. "We'll have to worry about saving the world later."

"Aye aye, Captain."

The kid snapped to his version of attention, and actually fired off a pretty good imitation of a salute in his attempt to play along.

"Alright, punk, grab the other end of this tray, and try not to drop it this time."

Jimmy complied, taking the opposite end of the tray the cake was sitting on. Together, he and Benji placed the tray on a waiting trolley, and slowly began to make their way from the kitchen, towards the banquet room. As they cleared the double doors, a fresh round of sirens could be heard over the clatter of activity often associated with a busy restaurant. Together, they paused and watched through the front window as Range City police cruisers went speeding by.

Once they'd driven past, Jimmy turned to look at Benji, and with a sincerity the older man had not heard before said, "You know, something needs to be done. Somebody has to do something."

The kid's words struck a chord, and Benji nodded his head in agreement. As the second wave of sirens also began to fade away in the distance, he led the way to the banquet room.

Once the grand dessert had been delivered to the Councilman's family and friends, receiving a nice round of applause, Benji returned to his kitchen and began preparations for the next order. He had a hard time concentrating however; Jimmy's words continued to resonate in his mind.

"The kid's right, somebody does need to do something."

He could only shake his head in frustration once more, as he grabbed the ingredients to prepare his famous chocolate mousse.

CHAPTER 2

Evil Lurks

Meanwhile—across town in his secret underground lair—a sinister villain was also hard at work mixing ingredients. Though he was not trying to whip together some tasty dessert treat, he was instead attempting to perfect a mind control formula, a formula so insidious the unsuspecting populace of Range City would never know what hit them. A formula that when completed, would help him hatch a scheme that would make him rich beyond his wildest dreams.

The evil doer laughed maniacally at his plot, the shrill sound of his cackle echoing faintly through the cavernous room. Rubbing his hands together in anticipatory glee, he refocused his attention on the mad scientist chemistry set laid out before him. Liquids bubbled and popped as they began to boil in their heated tubes, while beakers filled with steaming liquids of various colors gave off such a foul stench that even the earthy, moldy smell of the cavern would have been a welcome relief.

It was only a matter of time before he would be able to set his plan in motion, and the beautiful part was no one would be able to stop him. This would be the perfect crime, and even if it was not, this city had become so indifferent and corrupt he was sure he would still get away with it. Before it was all said and done, the citizens of this cesspool of a town would cower in their homes. *They will all bow down before me, and I will rule this city with an iron fist.*

Again, the sound of a high pitched cackle filled the cavern. Being evil was so much fun! His eyes sparkled with madness as he stared into the greenish liquid slowly dripping into a fresh beaker.

If this batch proved to be the correct configuration, it would be bad guy time.

Without warning however, the glass beaker shattered, spraying the villain with slime-green liquid and tiny shards of glass. As quickly as it began, the squealing laughter ceased. Where mere seconds before the echoing sounds of glee were bouncing around the cavern walls like a crazed pinball, there was now only silence. It was as though a switch had been flipped, turning the underground lair from a jubilant rumpus room into a deathly still tomb.

In a moment of exasperation, the unknown villain swept his arm out, crashing through his laboratory destroying everything in his path. The cacophony of breaking glass replaced the silence, followed by a wailing which would have put any two-year-old child to shame. Much like the liquids of his experiment, his frustration was boiling over.

Looking down at the broken remnants of his most recent failure, he took a deep breath. Once he had his violent temper under control, he turned, and walked out of the cavern. He would have to restock his supplies before beginning again. The only thing this setback had really cost him was time, which was the one thing he had in abundance.

Glancing at his watch, he realized it was almost time to go to work; it was important for him to maintain his cover. There could be absolutely no signs of impropriety if his plan was going to succeed. He hated the menial tasks he had to perform in order to keep the charade up, but it was a necessary evil.

A necessary evil, he liked the sound of that. He himself was a necessary evil a corrupt town like Range City deserved. He would be the worm living in the core of this rotten apple. Oh, the good times he was going to have at the expense of others! *The way this town is going, it will be easy pickings*. He would merely be the vulture feasting on the decaying carcass.

Range City had deteriorated into a haven of criminal activity, and he had no desire to be left behind. In fact, he planned on being the top dog, the head honcho, the evilest of the evil. He had a perfect plan, and shortly, he would unleash his unthinkable plot onto the unsuspecting populace. The laughter returned as these thoughts ricocheted through his dastardly mind.

After making his way back to the surface, he quickly donned the uniform of his undercover persona. He pulled his keys from a hook by the door, and stepped out into the hot and humid afternoon sun. The glare hurt his eyes, so he slipped on a pair of dark mirrored sunglasses.

After unlocking the door of the large white vehcile in the driveway, he climbed in and fired up the engine, roaring to life with a fury all its own. He made his way towards the town he planned on robbing blind; the poor fools had no idea what was in store for them.

Upon entering Range City limits and the first street lined with houses where children were at play, he reached over to the dashboard and flipped a switch. The sound of circus-style music began blaring out of the large speakers sitting on the truck's roof. He slowed to a crawl and watched as children flocked to him as if by magic, like moths to a flame.

Yes, it won't be long now, he thought to himself, smiling with an evil intensity. Once his formula was perfected, the foolish citizens of this town would be his. They would all kneel before him. They would live in fear of… the Ice Cream Man!

CHAPTER 3
Closing Time

At 10 p.m., after the last patrons of Chez Louis' Ristoranté—a young couple out for a late dinner—walked out the front door, the manager flipped the open sign to closed, and turned the lock, bolting the front door tightly.

The busboys went about gathering up the dirty dishes and taking then into the kitchen to be washed. The maitre d' floated from table to table quickly blowing out the decorative candles that added to the ambiance and quaint charm. The waitresses were sitting at their customary table near the kitchen entrance, talking and laughing as they counted their tips. This same scene played itself out every night at closing time, almost as if it were scripted in some way and the employees of the restaurant were merely actors playing their parts.

Benji took it all in, watching through the circular windows set into the upper portion of the double doors that separated the dining room from the kitchen. He loved this place. The kitchen was his world and the only place he felt at peace. This restaurant, and on a grander scale, this city, had become his home.

"Hey Cap," Jimmy called from behind him. "You plan on helping us get this place cleaned up or are you going to stare at the waitresses all night?"

He dropped his head and smirked. *One of these days I'm going to have to put that young pup in his place.* In the mean time however, he had to admit Jimmy was right. As head chef, one of his duties was to make sure the kitchen was in order and ready for the restaurant's opening the next night.

"If you haven't forgotten, my young assistant, I am in charge here, and if I choose to stare at the beauty that is the waitress staff while you slave away cleaning my kitchen, well then that's my prerogative. Rank does have its privileges you know."

The sound of groans followed by chuckles filled the kitchen as the four-man cooking staff, including Jimmy, went back to work. The comforting sounds of sous chefs going about their duties returned.

Benji watched them for a few moments as they worked diligently at cleaning the kitchen, before joining them. Yes, he was in charge, the Captain so to speak, but he had responsibilities and a job to do as well. Together, they all worked like a well-oiled machine, and talk was kept to a minimum as everyone focused on their assigned tasks. It reminded him quite fondly of being in the Army; everyone knew what their job was, and did it to the best of their abilities without question.

His own task at the moment was to prep for tomorrow night's dinner special, linguini in a clam and mushroom sauce. The linguini, like all pasta at Chez Louis Ristoranté, was made fresh daily by hand. The mushrooms needed to be diced as well. He went about his business, completing these two duties as he listened to the hustle and bustle of his staff.

After an hour or so, the clatter of the busy cooks lessened as the kitchen was once again clean and ready for action. The chrome and stainless steel of various utensils and counter tops alongside the monstrous ovens gleamed in the glow of the overhead lights. The dishes sparkled like precious gems after having been intensely scrubbed by both man and machine. It was quitting time.

The entire restaurant staff had been systematically trickling out, on their way home or out for a night of fun with friends, until he and Jimmy were the only two left. This was not unusual as he was almost always the last to leave, and Jimmy usually stuck around to keep him company. It had become so commonplace in fact, the manager had given him his own set of keys, and he had taken it upon himself to make sure the restaurant was locked up each night.

"Another day another dollar, eh Cap?"

Benji looked over at his co-worker, only to see him leaning casually against the large sink with his arms folded across his chest.

"This day isn't quite over, Jimmy boy, so don't be too worried about spending the dollar you think you've earned just yet."

"Whaddya mean?" the younger chef asked confused. "Everything is done, so lock this baby up and let's roll."

Benji smiled at his assistant knowingly, then nodded his head in the general direction of several plastic bags piled on top of each other near the service entrance door at the rear of the kitchen.

"I'm pretty sure those bags aren't going to take themselves out to the dumpster."

"Oh man, you've got to be kidding me, I'm a chef not a garbage man."

He had to laugh out loud at the sound of utter dejection in Jimmy's voice, and though he did feel a slight pang of guilt at finding such humor in his protégé's misery, it passed quickly as he recalled the many instances he himself had been on the receiving end of one of the young man's verbal barbs.

"Well, at least for tonight it would seem you get to be both. Think of this as a promotion."

The look the youngest member of his cooking staff fired back at him brought on a new round of laughter.

"Gee, Boss, thanks. Does it come with a raise?" the young chef responded, his voice dripping with sarcasm.

"There sure is," Benji responded, with an equal amount of sarcasm. "You 'raise' your arms, and carry those bags to the dumpster."

A groan of contempt was the reply he received.

"Tell ya what, you get started hauling those bags out, and I'll come help as soon as I finish putting these mushrooms in the refrigerator. If I don't get them put up soon, they'll go bad. I would hate to have to blame that on you," he joked, tossing a wink his assistant's way.

"Yeah, well don't take your time or anything."

Benji continued laughing at his friend's over exaggerated distress at his predicament. Simple moments of camaraderie like these between himself and Jimmy helped him forget about the sirens from earlier in the evening, and the larger problem of Range City's ever increasing crime rate.

He quickly finished refrigerating the diced mushrooms, and returned to help Jimmy take out the trash. He had to admit he was getting tired, and even though he loved this restaurant and even more so this kitchen, he was ready to go home.

At that moment, Fate decided to intervene.

CHAPTER 4

Fate Steps In

Benji walked over to the bags of trash, bending over so he could get a better grip, when a flashing glint of metal caught his eye. Lying on the floor was a large, three-pronged serving fork. It must have fallen during the clamor and commotion of the evening clean up, and had been forgotten.

He reached down and picked the utensil up, thinking he would wash it and put it away with the others, when a sharp cry and the sound of a struggle from the alley behind the restaurant caught his attention. The same alley Jimmy had carried trash bags out to a few minutes earlier.

He never hesitated; the soldier in him came out, and he barged through the back door with abandon. He was pretty sure the cry had not come from Jimmy, the voice was too high pitched, like that of a young woman. Whatever was going on in the alley, Jimmy was more than likely caught right in the middle of it. He had no idea what was happening down there, but it had to be trouble. The ear piercing cry he had heard was not one of happy surprise, but one of complete terror.

What he saw stopped him dead in his tracks. A man was standing in front of the dumpster on the opposite side of the alley, directly across from the back door. The guy had one arm wrapped tightly around the neck of an extremely frightened looking woman. In his other hand he was holding a large caliber handgun, one he had pointed squarely at Jimmy. Benji was struck by how young the gunman was. *What is this city coming to, if even the youth turned to a life of crime?*

To his credit, Jimmy did not look frightened. He was standing statue-still, staring intently at their dangerous visitor with the gun. The girl on the other hand, was crying openly. The look in her eye was one of pleading for help.

"Don't come any closer, or your friend here is a dead man," the crook with the gun said menacingly.

"Look dude, we don't want any trouble."

The sound of Jimmy's voice broke the spell the shock of the situation caused. Benji was proud of the kid for being able to keep his cool and remain calm; he knew from his experiences in the Army, this was no time for rash decisions and brash attempts at heroics. With that knowledge secure in his mind, he began running through various scenarios on how to resolve their current dilemma. The problem however, was every version he came up with ended in disaster.

"Look guy, Jimmy's right. We don't want any trouble, so why don't you let the girl go. Take whatever you want, and just leave. There'll be no questions asked."

The girl suddenly stopped sobbing. She went from being a young, terrified victim to a calm, woman in control, in the blink of an eye. Without the tears and hysterics, she started to look familiar. Benji was stunned when he recognized her as a part-time waitress from the restaurant.

"Are these the two you were telling us about?" the gunman asked, letting go of his pretend hostage.

"Yeah, they're it," the former victim answered. "There's nobody else inside."

The whole scene had become surreal. This had been nothing more than a set up, a pathetic scheme to rob the restaurant. The waitress had been a decoy to get he and Jimmy outside where they could be contained while the robbery was being committed. The back door was hanging wide open so all the crooks had to do was waltz right in and clean the place out. He felt like a complete fool for falling for such an obvious ploy, then saw the wicked look in the gunman's eye, and knew things were about to go from bad to worse.

"Well then, let's quit screwing around and get to it."

The gunman refocused his attention on Jimmy, staring at the young sous chef for a couple of seconds, aimed quickly, and fired. The blast from the gun was deafening as it echoed through the air.

Everything seemed to go deathly still.

Benji watched in horror as Jimmy spun in a complete circle, like the kid was doing a pirouette in a kind of macabre dance. Everything else seemed to move in slow motion. He could not even bring himself to call out to Jimmy. He could only watch as his friend crumbled to the dirty pavement of the alley, where he lay unmoving.

Suddenly, all of his senses came alive, and the night became crystal clear; he could actually smell the pungent odor of burnt gunpowder from the discharged weapon. The steel of the serving fork he still held in his hand became so cold it caused a burning sensation. In an odd sort of way, he had never felt so alive. He continued to watch with pristine clarity as the shooter brought the pistol to bear and pointed it directly at his chest. If he did not think of something quickly, Benji knew he would be joining Jimmy on the cold ground of the alley.

He did not hesitate. With reflexes honed by the finest training the Army Corp of Engineers had to offer, he gripped the large fork loosely by the handle, and threw it with uncommon accuracy. The utensil flew straight as an arrow through the air, striking the gunman in the wrist, causing the crook to release his weapon.

The attacker yelped in pain as the gun fell to the ground. Seeing the shooter was now unarmed, Benji prepared to charge in hopes of tackling the would-be robber so he could be immobilized. He was so focused on getting his hands on Jimmy's shooter, he never noticed the third member of the gang, one who had been waiting in the shadows wielding a wooden baseball bat, until it was too late.

Before Benji could even take a step towards the wounded attacker, the third member swung the bat with such force, it would have made Albert Pujols proud. The bat connected squarely with the back of Benji's head with a sickening thud.

An explosion of bright light flashed before his eyes. There was a moment of intense pain followed by a strange numbness. He felt as if he was suddenly floating through the air, like a feather caught in the wind. The feeling was not all that unpleasant, until he landed face-first on the unforgiving pavement. He heard what he thought was laughter, then nothing as everything was swallowed by the blackness of unconsciousness.

CHAPTER 5

A Formula Perfected

With his regular evening route completed, the evil villain known only as the Ice Cream Man was back at his secret hideout, located in the old power building on the edge of Range City. Over the past few months he'd secretly converted the underground basement of the vacant building into a high-tech laboratory. It was there he worked diligently to bring his evil scheme to fruition.

His eyes seemed to shine in the dimly lit basement lab, matching those of the rats, the other inhabitants of his subterranean lair. The glint in his eyes hinted at madness, but was really more along the lines of pure evil genius. A look of fierce determination remained on his villainous face while he concentrated on mixing the ingredients to his precious formula.

Luck had been on his side the day the formula came into his possession, perhaps nothing short of divine intervention. Oh, the law would probably call it stealing, but how could you steal what was rightfully yours to begin with?

Those fools with their secrets at the government labs thought he was nothing more than a guinea pig for their experiments. He'd shown them. Thinking him a simple test subject, they had unknowingly increased his intellect to almost super-human levels. They stupidly believed him to be just another willing participant, so he bided his time. When the moment presented itself, he seized the opportunity, and escaped from their clutches.

While making his escape, he'd hid in one of the many offices where—lying on a desk like the Holy Grail waiting to be claimed—a print out of a formula lay on the desk. He quickly snatched it up, stowing it away as he made his getaway. Those fools had no idea what they had created; with his now genius level intellect, he'd recognized the potential greatness the formula could have.

It did not take him long to assume a new identity and set up shop. Range City, with its corrupt officials and wondrously high crime rate, was the perfect place to locate his base of operations. The city itself would offer him the perfect opportunity to master the formula's intricacies and test its effects.

And that brought him back to the present. He had tweaked the original formula, increasing the potency ten fold. Therein lied the problem, however, as it had become unstable. It was a matter of finding the right amount of Thiamine Mononitrate, the special ingredient that gave the formula its potency. Luckily, he was able to find it in abundance, hidden in ordinary vanilla ice cream. The next step was heating the mixed ingredients to perfection over a period of time.

His failures over the last few weeks were due to heating the precious liquid the formula produced too quickly, but every failure had brought him closer to his goal. He thought the last batch would be the one to finally allow him to put his plans of domination into effect, but alas, it was not to be. It was the closest he had come and he was now ready to try once more.

With concentration mixed with reverence, dedication, and obsession, he began combining the volatile ingredients. The stench of sulfur filled the cavernous basement as the different items began intermingling with each other. He held each component as if it were a piece of centuries-old fine China that might shatter if gripped too tightly.

Mold from a blueberry muffin, the rind of a rotten grapefruit, cherry flavored cough syrup, a vial of slobber from an English bulldog, and a sheet of math homework featuring multiplication problems written in number 2 pencil were all added accordingly. The Ice Cream Man smiled wickedly with childish glee as each item dropped into the increasingly foul liquid with a satisfying hiss. He was as happy as a kid on Christmas morning, stirring his vile concoction with a dirty spoon.

Lastly came the final yet most important ingredient, Thiamine Mononitrate, which he got from a scoop of vanilla ice cream that had been melted down in a separate beaker. He would then heat it to a roiling boil, and immediately pour it into the glass beaker containing the rest of the formula.

He was ready to do that exact thing right now. The sound of bubbling liquids told him it was ready, so he slipped on an oversized, black industrial rubber glove, snatched the super heated vial of the precious liquid, and poured it into the awaiting mixture.

As soon as the most important of ingredients touched the liquid already brewing, it turned a bright neon green. An eerie steam wafted out of the vial, and seemed to fill the basement with its presence. A sickly-sweet smell replaced that of the sulfur.

Now came the crucial part, the heating of the complete formula. For the mind control properties to work effectively, it had to be warmed up to 120 degrees Fahrenheit, but it had to be done slowly. One second too quick and the formula would not stabilize properly, resulting in a mini explosion much like his last attempt.

He'd heated the steaming liquid for twenty-two minutes to reach the desired temperature. It had been two minutes too long evidently, the result of which was he had ended up covered in green slime when the formula exploded. He had been so close, but in the end the result was yet another failure.

This time he had a great idea—an epiphany if you will—to help time the heating process. He figured it would take twenty minutes to hit the desired 120 degree temperature and have the formula stabilize. To make sure he stayed in that time parameter, he would order a pizza from Domino's. According to their advertisement, if his order was not delivered in twenty minutes, it would be free. This way when his pizza arrived the time would be perfect, and if by chance it was not, then at least his dinner would be free. It most definitely paid to have the brain power of an evil genius.

He grabbed his cell phone and quickly dialed the number for Domino's Pizza, a number he had memorized in preparation for this moment. When the sound of a kid answered on the other end, he did not wait for a greeting, but instead blurted out his order.

"I want a medium double anchovy and mushroom pizza. Oh, and a liter of diet soda."

When the kid on the other end confirmed the order, the Ice Cream Man flipped a switch on the heating element. If his assumptions were correct, by the time the pizza arrived the formula would be ready. He trembled with excited anticipation as he hung up, and slipped his phone back in his pocket.

The wait was excruciating. Though it was only twenty minutes, it felt like an eternity. He put the old axiom "a watched pot never boils" to the test as he stared intently at the formula. He was prepared to move quickly and leap from his perch to save it at the first sign of trouble. So far though, things were going according to his plan. The slow heating process was working perfectly.

He was focused so intently on the glass container, that when the buzzer went off, signaling someone was at his front door ringing the doorbell, it startled him so badly he fell off his stool. He grabbed the side of the lab table to pull himself up. Once he was back to his feet, he turned the heating element off.

The buzzer went off again, but he ignored it. Instead, his full attention was focused on the now completely stable formula. He was so excited he was trembling. There was only one thing left for him to check.

He scanned the lab table until his gaze fell on the item he was looking for. He snatched the meat thermometer up, and slipped the pointed end into the vile green ooze. After a few seconds, the temperature gauge showed a glorious 120 degrees. It was perfect.

The buzzer went off a third time, breaking the spell the success of his precious formula had caused. It was all he could do to tear himself away; if he did not go pay for his pizza however, the delivery driver would leave, and he would not only be left hungry without any dinner, but he would lose his very first test subject.

He grabbed the rapidly cooling beaker, and made his way out of the sub-basement. He had constructed a tunnel from the abandoned power plant where he had set up his laboratory, to a small cottage located on the same lot. It was there he made his residence.

He rushed back up the tunnel, through the trap door opening up in his bedroom, and through the rest of the cottage to the door. The delivery driver, a high school kid trying to look cool, was walking back to his car. The Ice Cream Man smiled evilly; a young teenager, this was even better.

"Excuse me, I'm sorry I didn't answer sooner. I was in the... bathroom."

"Yeah, man, I have better things to do than stand around your creepy yard ringing the door bell all night," the delivery driver responded sarcastically.

"Again, I apologize. Why don't you come inside, and I'll get your money."

"Sure dude, but you better hurry up. It's hot out here."

The Ice cream Man smiled knowingly. "You can have something cold to drink while I find my wallet."

"You have a Pepsi in this shack of yours?" the teenage driver asked as he walked into the cottage.

The evil villain looked down at the vial of green liquid he was holding in his hand, and chuckled. "I have something different, something you might like even better."

CHAPTER 6

Just a Dream... Isn't It?

At first there was nothing, just an overwhelming blackness covering him like an comfortable old blanket, keeping him warm. Then the darkness began to shift and move.

At the start, it was a slight movement around the edges, slowly picking up speed as it began to swirl in a circular motion. Faster and faster the darkness twirled until it was a maelstrom of activity, a vicious whirlpool threatening to suck him down into its terrifying, bottomless depths.

The constant spinning sensation began to make him feel sick to his stomach, the uneasy feeling of being on the verge of having to throw up. He wanted to lift his arm to help steady his balance, perhaps put a stop to the infernal movement, but for some reason his limbs would not respond. There was only the swirling blackness.

Panic began to creep up on him as a sense of helpless dread. He knew he was in trouble and more than likely hurt, though how bad he was unsure, and for the life of him he could not remember what happened. At the moment, his memory had deserted him much like the control over his extremities.

For the briefest of instances he feared he was dead, the black nothingness signifying the deepest void of them all, but he quickly dismissed that notion. If this was indeed death, why did he feel a deep, centered, purpose? He had an almost overpowering sensation of a job left undone, a task left incomplete, leaving him with the knowledge of having work to do, a mission to complete, a destiny to fulfill.

At that exact moment the blackness started to evaporate. As quickly as it began swirling, it dissolved into a myriad of colors. Those colors slowly began to build into shapes, and eventually, the shapes formed images. The images, fleeting at first, finally settled into focus.

Benji was surprised to see the images were of him, as though someone had secretly followed him with a video camera during periods of his life, and he was now watching the resulting movie. It was a surreal moment, and once again he had a quick flash of fear that he was dead. Maybe the legend of seeing your life flash before your eyes was true, and this was his time. If this was true, then why would the images be starting after he was dead? It could only mean he was still among the living, but for how long was anybody's guess.

As the images continued to play themselves out, he was startled to see many were of him while he was with the Army Corps of Engineers. He saw himself utilizing a variety of resources to help complete different missions. He watched as he learned how to manipulate metals to create new tools and weapons. While the trip through his past continued to play, he felt an underlying sense of something more, as if he were being shown these images for a reason, for a purpose far greater.

While he pondered the meaning of it all, the images shifted. He now saw himself work his way through culinary school, watching again as a variety of utensils were used to accomplish a given task. Still, hanging out there like a huge neon sign trying to get his attention, was the powerful sensation of a larger purpose. It was all so confusing. What could these two completely unrelated times in his life have in common?

Once again the images wavered and changed; he watched as the events leading up to the blackness were shown. He watched helplessly as Jimmy was shot, and felt gut-wrenching guilt overwhelm him. In all that was happening right now, he had forgotten his friend and young protégé had also been injured.

A sharp, white-hot pain brought his attention back to the pictures playing on the strange movie screen in his mind. This time the scene was in slow motion, showing the moment where he used the large serving fork as a means to disarm the attacker. It seemed to rewind, and then start again. It was like watching a picture in picture television option, as the first two scenarios of this bizarre dream were being shown in the bottom two corners of his imagined screen. Then all three scenes converged into one image, clearing up all confusion and answering all of his questions.

A large image of him, armed with utensils manipulated from his training, fighting the evil denizens overriding Range City. Benji knew, and for the first time in his life, he understood what the nagging feeling of a deeper purpose to his life meant. This town had become his home, and the citizens his friends. The criminal element Range City was infested with seeped into his comfort zone by violating his sanctuary at the restaurant. Something had to be done. The people of this fair city needed help. They needed a beacon of light to give them hope. They needed a hero.

He opened his eyes only to be blinded by the glare of the afternoon sun shining through an open window. He had no idea where he was, or how he had gotten here. He had a horrible headache, especially in the back of his head where he had been hit, and still felt some queasiness left over from the powerful visions he had experienced.

Though he was hurt, he could not remember a time he felt so invigorated. His mission was now crystal clear; he knew he had a lot of work to do, and he could not wait to get started.

Benji took a quick survey of his surroundings and realized he was in a hospital room. He lifted his right hand to his head and felt the heavy gauze bandage wrapped there. He wanted to sit up, but common sense held him in place. The sound of a door opening alerted him to a visitor.

"Ah, Mr. Winters I see you're finally awake," a concerned voice said from the foot of the bed where the doctor had stopped.

"Is Jimmy okay?" Benji asked hopefully.

There was an ominous pause before the doctor answered. "No, Mr. Winters, I'm afraid he's not. We did everything we could, but Jimmy's wound was too severe, and he didn't make it."

The determination and exhilaration of finally figuring out what his purpose in life truly was came crashing down. Jimmy was dead, and nothing else seemed to matter.

Lying there in bed, stunned, feeling guilty and miserably helpless, the pain hit him again, and he closed his eyes, wincing until the pain started to lessen. The images from earlier flashed through his befuddled brain, reminding him of the greater need. When he opened his eyes again, the determination was back. He knew without a shadow of a doubt what he had to do.

The dream had given him focus. The images lit the path of his destiny. He had a purpose, and with Jimmy's death a horrible reality, he most definitely had the motivation. He would be the hero Range City needed. The dream, or divine intervention, or whatever it was, had put him on this path and he meant to see it through with every fiber of his being.

Chapter 7

Saying Goodbye With a Promise

Three days later, Benji was released from the Range City Memorial Hospital. He was still feeling the after effects of the concussion. The physical pain was bearable however compared to the emotional trauma he was still suffering from.

Most people are happy when they finally get to leave a hospital. It is usually a joyous time signaling a recovery of some sort. Not for him though, as this day was also the day his friend Jimmy was going to be laid to rest. Benji was going to leave the hospital and go directly to the funeral. It was not exactly a time for celebration.

The strange vision was still lingering in the back of his mind as he made his way out to the cemetery for the graveside service. Knowing he was finally going to do something good about the crime problem did not lessen the sting of Jimmy's death. Having to go and say a final goodbye to a person so young and so full of potential made him want to cry. He was not sure if it was his concussion or the pain of the loss of his friend, but he felt as if he might be sick.

James "Jimmy" Davis was laid to rest at Range City Serenity Gardens Cemetery. It was a bright, sunny day, in complete contrast to the dark mood Benji was in. He was glad to see all the employees of Chez Louis Ristoranté were there, along with several of the restaurant's regular customers.

The service was beautiful, if indeed such a somber event can be described in such a manner. Many tears were shed, and many hugs were shared in comfort among those who knew Jimmy best. Much like his life, the service was too short, but in the end what more could anyone say. No matter how you looked at it, his death was a tragedy. The kid had lived his life to the fullest, and now it was time for those he left behind to get on with their own.

With the service over, the mourners began filtering out, and Benji suddenly found himself alone. He stared at the beautiful cherry wood casket, gold in-lay running around the edge, and knew it was time to say a final goodbye to the kid he considered his best friend.

"I'm so sorry Jimmy. I feel like I let you down, and I can't figure out for the life of me why it had to be your time. It's just not fair." He paused, fighting back a lump of emotion building in his throat. He was hurting like never before from an overwhelming sense of grief, but he was determined not to cry. He wanted to be strong for his friend.

"I've had some time to do some serious thinking. I know now what I have to do. It's something I should have done long ago. If I had, maybe you would still be here."

Again he paused to settle his emotions and gather his thoughts.

"You were the one to challenge me about something needing to be done to save this city. Well, I am here to tell you something will be done. This city needs someone to take charge and be a hero. I am ready to accept your challenge, and I will be that hero. This I promise you Jimmy. I promise you will have justice."

With his vow still hanging in the air, he took a long deep breath, feeling the steel resolve of his promise flow through his veins. He never felt so sure about anything in his life. The last promise to his friend energized his determination. With one final look at Jimmy's resting place, Benji turned and took the first step to a much larger journey. He walked out of the Range City Serenity Garden Cemetery with his head held high, and the sun shining brightly on his back.

It was time to go to work. He had a vow to fulfill. It was time to be a hero.

CHAPTER 8
The Perfect Plan

The initial test had worked perfectly.

The unsuspecting pizza delivery driver was akin to the trusting fly entering the spider's parlor. The foolish youth was easily duped into drinking a healthy dose of the mind control formula. It worked its way through the young driver's system, and took hold with its insidious iron grip almost immediately.

The fiendish Ice Cream Man looked on with selfish glee as his test subject gulped down the formula. Within seconds, he could see the changes in his guest's demeanor. The glossing over of the eyes, giving them a sleepy dreamy look, the slumping shoulders, and the look of almost complete peaceful serenity were a dead giveaway the formula was working.

He could not believe the moment was finally at hand. The months of preparation, along with all of the trial and errors, had culminated to this simple little test. If this was successful, then everything would be ready for him to become an extremely wealthy villain.

As the delivery driver leaned casually against the kitchen counter, still looking serene and peaceful, the Ice Cream Man crossed to the table where a CD player sat, waiting to play its own part in his evil little experiment. The playful smile vanished from his face as nervousness took hold. This was the moment of truth; success or failure of his master plan hinged on the next crucial moments. Not wanting to waste any more time, he reached over, and hit the play button.

The quiet kitchen was quickly filled with the sound of festive pipe organ carnival music. The effect on the delivery driver was instantaneous. His body, which mere seconds before had been relaxed, jerked to rigid attention. He stared at the CD player with his utmost attention. He had the appearance of a steadfast soldier, standing before a commanding officer to receive the orders for an all-important mission. In actuality, this was not far from the truth.

After a few more seconds of being at erect attention, the pizza delivery driver turned, and walked out the front door without looking back. He walked straight to his vehicle, and sped away into the early evening. The sudden shift in the young driver's demeanor would have appeared quite out of the ordinary to the average bystander, but to the evil genius of the Ice Cream Man it was poetry in motion.

He had known perfecting the formula was only part of the problem. There was also the dilemma of how to deliver his instructions once his minions were under his direct control. Again, he found the solution in his own assumed persona. The annoying music he was forced to play as he made his rounds around Range City was the perfect distribution system.

The music was loud, and he blared it the whole time he was selling his frozen treats to the unsuspecting populace of Range City. With his evil brilliance, it had been nothing for him to place subliminal messages onto the CD. When the youth would fall under his control from the formula-laced ice cream he would soon be selling, they would become receptive to the messages hidden in the music he played. It was the perfect plan.

He had waited for hours, and now there was one thing left to check on before everything would fall into place. He needed to see if his test subject had followed through with his instructions. Glaring at his watch noticing the time was five minutes until 11 P.M., he turned on his television to catch the upcoming local news. After surfing through several channels, he finally found what he was looking for. He laughed out loud as he watched, hearing the Channel 4 anchorman describing the scene as it unfolded.

"Citizens of Range City were caught by surprise this evening as local teenager and Domino's Pizza Delivery Driver,

Todd Stevens, drove his delivery vehicle, still loaded with pizza orders, onto the front lawn of Mayor Martinez's personal residence. Stevens then removed all of his clothing, and began doing cannonballs into the large fountain, the centerpiece of the Mayor's lawn.

Police were immediately called to the scene where they quickly subdued and apprehended the young man who gave up without a struggle. When asked why he was displaying this unusual behavior, Mr. Stevens only reply was 'The music told me too.' "

It had worked. Everything was ready for him to make his move and put this most perfect of plans into motion. As he got up and began walking back to his secret underground lab to make preparations, he began laughing hysterically.

The evil villain, the Ice Cream Man, was still laughing as he entered his lab to finalize a plan that would soon rock the foundation of Range City to its very core.

CHAPTER 9
The Right Tools for the Right Job

Benji couldn't sleep that night, after the funeral. He decided to take a drive in an effort to clear his head. Wandering aimlessly all over town, he looked for the answers to the multitude of questions playing out in his head. He knew what he wanted to do, and with an even stronger conviction he knew what he must do. He had the necessary drive, now all he needed were the right tools. For him to become Range City's hero, protector, and possible savior, he needed the equipment he knew best. He pulled over and parked.

An eerie feeling of déjà vu washed over Benji, and a shiver crawled his spine as he found himself standing in the back alley of the Chez Louis Ristoranté. He felt as if he had come full circle in this strange sojourn destiny placed him on; a mere few feet away was the place where fate had intervened, where Jimmy's life had been taken.

He stayed rooted to the ground, afraid to approach any closer. He understood that with his next step, he would be on a path of no return, a path forcing him to take up the challenge and responsibility of becoming the town's champion. He had a feeling his whole life had been leading up to this moment. His stints in the military and his training as a chef were simply the acts of a much larger performance that hadn't as of yet played itself to the end. With the next step, he would be placed on some cosmic trail he was preordained to follow. It was a daunting task, but one he was more than willing to accept.

A slight wind kicked up, cooling off the lazy heat and humidity of early evening. The breeze caused the yellow police tape still ringing the crime scene to flutter and flap. The crisp whipping sound pulled him out of his self-reflections, and focused his attention to the here and now. He felt a bit ashamed for having stalled when there was so much work yet to be done.

Reaching into the pocket of his jeans, he pulled out the key to the restaurant's back door, the same key given to him by the manager of the restaurant as a sign of trust. Unfortunately he would now have to break that trust if he was going to be able to fulfill his vow. It somehow seemed wrong for something he knew in his heart to be so right to start out like this. There was simply no other alternative however; everything he needed to help further his cause in helping this city was lying right beyond the old metal door.

Still an active crime scene, the police had not yet caught the perpetrators. According to official reports, the crooks ransacked the restaurant as well as robbed the place. The trio of criminals had left he and Jimmy for dead while they made off with a few dollars in an attempt to satisfy their greed. This was the catalyst he needed to get himself moving. Without a second thought, he ducked under the police tape and made his way to the back door.

Another unnerving shiver racked his body as he stepped over the chalked outlines where he and Jimmy had lain, the place where Jimmy had taken his last breath. It had only been a few short days since the attack, and his head still ached from the concussion while his heart burned in pain from the loss of his friend. He knew his head would eventually heal, but the agony of Jimmy's murder would more than likely linger on and haunt him for the rest of his life. The whole thing still seemed completely surreal.

Hearing the tell-tale clicking of the tumblers in the lock falling into place was comforting. He gave a hard tug on the door and with a protesting groan, the door swung open.

The interior of the restaurant was dark and full of shadows. The sun was starting to rise, which meant his time was limited. He hoped to get in, grab what he wanted, and get out again before anyone was the wiser. It was time to get to work, except instead of cooking gourmet meals, he would in essence be using the utensils to cook up some much needed justice for the citizens of Range City.

He knew the kitchen area like it was the back of his own hand. Even in the meager light, he was sure he would be able to get around fairly easy, locating the objects of his desire. This place was his home away from home, or at least it had been, once upon a time. The crooks who attacked him not only robbed the money from the safe, they had stolen the good memories and peaceful feelings this place held for him.

The first thing he did was head to the cleaning and supply closet located directly across from the back door. On his way, he stepped over several items the crooks tossed aside in their hurry to find valuables; the site of the damage done to his beloved kitchen made his heart ache anew. He opened the unlocked door, and with practiced ease located the large, heavy duty bags used to store the rags and dish towels before they were taken to be laundered. He figured three bags would do the trick, knowing he could always come back for more if need be.

Shaking the bag open and taking a quick survey of the kitchen area, he was not quite sure where to start. The glint of light bouncing off the metal industrial-sized wash basins caught his eye, and he decided it would be best to start there.

He made his way through the obstacle course of debris, saddened when he saw all of his precious utensils thrown rather haphazardly over the cleaning station. These same utensils had been the tools he used to create his culinary masterpieces, now it was time for these tools to be put to an even more important use – justice for the citizens of Range City.

He smiled as he grabbed various items of silverware and placed them in the canvas bag. He took everything he could find; all of the spoons, forks, and knives in their various sizes were taken, along with tongs, meat thermometers, and hand-held mixers. He moved through each area until he had covered the entire kitchen and the canvas bag was filled.

Half-carrying and half-dragging the bag to the open rear door, Benji deposited it in the back alley. The silverware made a chiming sound as they banged together. He smiled and wiped the sweat from his brow before heading back inside.

He followed a similar routine with the second large bag. This time however, he filled it with every pot and pan he could locate. From large stewing pots, to various frying pans, to heavy duty cookie and baking sheets, he did not discriminate and took them all. He also grabbed every size lid he could find. They all went into the bag to be used for the greater good of the city.

When it, too, was full, he set it outside next to the packed silverware. The only difference was instead of a chiming sound, this bag made a loud clanging when it was deposited on the hard concrete of the alley.

After dragging out the heavy second bag, Benji noticed the light from the sun was brightening fast. He would have to hurry if he was going to finish his task before someone would be likely to see; quick yet cautious as he did not want to leave anything he might need behind.

He took the third bag, and hurriedly finished his work. He threw in any odds and ends he thought might prove useful. Cooking oils, whisks, and anything made of stainless steel that was small enough to stuff into his bag. Lastly, he grabbed his favorite blue apron, still hanging on the peg by the door where he had left it on that last fateful evening.

Benji took one last look around, feeling an emptiness in the pit of his stomach as he realized this would likely be the last time he stepped foot into the kitchen which had been his second home. He had a new job now, one in which cooking and baking had no place, unless it was to whip up some truth with a side order of justice.

He laughed out loud at his joke before walking back to his truck, driving it around back to the alley, and quickly loaded the three bags into the back. He hopped back into the cab, started the engine, and with a final glance back over his shoulder, drove off to begin his new career as champion of Range City.

CHAPTER 10

Plans and Preparations

Benji drove through town on his way back home. The sun was rising, and Range City was aglow with the soft light. The peacefulness was merely a charade, he knew, as a dark underbelly full of criminals and evil doers would soon slither out of their wretched holes to once again prey on the innocent. This was the motivation that drove him.

He made his way through town without incident. The police scanner lying on the seat next to him was oddly quiet as well. He had grown accustomed to its near constant squawking as a new crime was being discovered. This silence was a lull however, a calm before the storm. As if on cue, the police scanner came to life as the voice of a female dispatcher began calling all cars, a code 112 was in progress on the corner of Elm and Maple Streets.

He knew from experience that code 112 was a residential break and enter. Ever since crime had taken over Range City, he had taken to listening to the scanner, and was able to learn the codes the Range City Police Department used to communicate with each other. Now, in the distance, he could hear the faint sound of sirens as the police responded to the call and made their way to the scene.

The sirens quickly became a memory as he left the city limits, and made his way home, an old farmhouse about twenty miles outside of town. He enjoyed the quiet and solitude the location provided, and after a long night of work he would enjoy coming home to unwind and relax. Now however, he was returning home with a new purpose, and a new career.

After leaving the Army, he settled on Range City as the place to start a new life. He fell in love with the old farmhouse the first time the realtor had shown it to him. It needed lots of work, and he was able to pick it up fairly cheap. The house sat on three acres of land which also included a barn, garage, and much to his delight, a fully operational machine shop.

He spent the better part of his first year splitting his time between the restaurant and remodeling his new house. He truly enjoyed working with his hands, and thanks to the Army Corps of Engineers he had the training and know-how to do all the work himself. What was once a decrepit old eyesore of a house, was now a beautiful and sprawling Victorian style home. If he wanted he could sell the place for ten times what he originally paid for it. That was the furthest thought from his mind however; the place and Range City had become his home, and even more important than that, this was where he would make his stand on the side of justice.

Once he pulled into his driveway, a quarter mile of twisting dirt road, he bypassed the house and barn, and headed straight for the machine shop. Over the time he lived here, he refurbished and updated the shop to the point it could now rival any professional shop in town. There was something so satisfying in creating things with your hands, the same reason he enjoyed being a chef so much. He would tinker around in the shop to help satisfy his growing hobbies; this shop would take on a new role now, as the place where the tools of justice would be created.

He parked the truck, and quickly unloaded the supplies he had taken from the restaurant, which joined several other bags already lined up inside the shop. These bags contained everything left over from his days as a captain in the army.

To be the true hero and champion this town needed, and quite frankly deserved, it would take combining the training of both his worlds, civilian chef and ex-army captain, into one overriding force. He had the desire, the motivation, and now he had the necessary implements to make it all happen.

34

The last component in his equation for success was time. Thanks to the crooks who destroyed the restaurant, he had time in abundance, and with his army pension, he really did not need to work, he only did so because of his love of the culinary arts. This worked in his favor as he could now devote his every waking hour to the completion of this all-important mission.

He was anxious to get started, to get the wheels of justice rolling, but he knew with this kind of undertaking he would need detailed and extensive planning. Some simple blue prints were already drawn up, along with a list of several new ideas and concepts. He wanted nothing more than to jump into the deep end of this project feet first; he understood the longer he took in getting ready the more time the criminals of Range City had to sink their devious claws into the innocent citizens and businesses, creating an environment that was simply unacceptable in his estimation.

The desire was strong, but unfortunately his body was still weak; he was not completely recovered from his wounds. To Benji, this was only a reminder of what the people of this city had to suffer through on a daily basis. He would not be good to anybody in the condition he was in at the moment. He needed rest if he was going to be able to maintain the energy level to see this through to the end. The headache left over from his concussion was affecting his eyesight, and he could not work the machines necessary to create the tools he needed.

He headed to the house, where he went straight to his bedroom, immediately drifting off into a deep sleep. He'd only planned on taking a cat nap, but exhaustion took hold and he slept straight through till morning, his dreams filled with ideas and concepts to help bring his plans to fruition.

When the sun rose the next morning, he was refreshed and ready to grab his destiny by the tail with both hands.

The same time Benji Winters found himself standing in the back alley of the Chez Louis' Ristoranté pondering his next move, the evil Ice Cream Man was setting his own vile plan into motion.

After perfecting his formula and testing its effectiveness, the villain was ready to make his ideas of his own grandeur become a reality.

Earlier in the day, with a truck loaded down with his special "spiked" vanilla ice cream, the Ice Cream Man made his way through Range City offering up his delicious desserts to the young citizens who could never get enough of his treats, especially on a hot summer day.

As the children came running, he would select the most appropriate candidates he felt would be able to meet his purposes, and serve them a nice heaping bowl of the special ice cream. He watched with interest as the mind control formula took hold, changing the unsuspecting customers from care free youth, into minions of evil.

He was on his third and last pass through town, the music containing the subliminal instructions for his new servants blaring through the speaker system attached to the roof of his vehicle. He had no doubt his minions were hearing the music, and it was only a matter of time before his seedlings of evil intent would begin to bear fruit.

The nefarious criminal known only as the Ice Cream Man stole a quick glance out the window, and watching as the sun finally set, decided it was time to return to his lair. He had guests to prepare for, after all. The Ice Cream Man giggled with delight as he sped through town.

Chapter 11

Hard at Work

The loud, grinding sound of a power sander interrupted the otherwise serene morning; the quick flashes of orange sparks could be seen raining down through the dirt smudged windows of the machine shop as Benji diligently focused on his newest creation. He had risen with the sun and after a light breakfast, was eager to get to work putting together the arsenal he would need to fight the good fight.

Many of the ideas he had concocted were simple, not requiring much work or manipulation to get the items ready for use. He had already finished several of these items in fact, and these were lying off to one side on a separate work bench. Most were utensils that only needed to be sharpened or honed to a fine piercing point. It was the more intricate designs that held his attention and required his deep concentration at the moment.

He felt almost like a blacksmith as he moved the sander across the large stainless steel baking pan he was currently working on. Guiding the sander back and forth across the pan, the metal had become as smooth as glass. He had big plans for this particular piece of metal, as he intended to use this not as a weapon of any kind, but as an important piece of personal protection.

A heavy, slurping, bubbling sound caught his attention. He turned to look at a large black cauldron sitting over an even larger flame. Placing the belt sander down on the bench, he walked over and peered inside, nodding in satisfaction.

Inside the cauldron was a thick, gray liquid. Many of the items he removed from the restaurant's kitchen were made of heavy duty stainless steel. Of those items, the ones he had no plans for utilizing as part of his arsenal, he placed in the black pot with the idea of melting them down. The result of this process was the dirty fluid he was now looking at.

Part of his training in the Army Corps of Engineers dealt with the manipulation of certain metals, and it was this knowledge he planned to put to good use once again. With the steel melted down, it could be molded or reformed into whatever he desired. Another key factor was how the liquid steel could be used to reinforce and strengthen many of his other creations.

He checked the heat source, making sure it would remain hot enough to keep the metal in a liquid state. Once he was satisfied everything was in order, he returned to his work bench. Sweat beaded on his brow, and he slowly wiped it off with the back of his arm. He had been hard at work for several hours now, and many of his ideas were starting to take shape.

Every available space on the walls of the machine shop was covered with blueprints, technical read-outs, and hand written notes. These plans were written on everything from sticky notes to legal pads to the back of paper plates. Once he committed himself to this cause, the ideas had come flooding out of his head. None of the things he thought up were too far-fetched for him, he believed anything could be possible. He dismissed none of them, and instead wrote them all down on whatever happened to be handy at the time. The result was the paper murals now lining the shop walls.

Benji felt good about the work already done, though it was just a drop in the bucket, as there was so much more to do. His mind was moving a mile a minute, the pot of coffee he had consumed only added to the whirlwind. All morning long he jumped from one project to the next, the easy items completed—like the sharpened three pronged forks—only fueled his desire to keep working. The idea to take a break never entered his mind.

There was so much more he needed to accomplish, the difficult tools he was going to need still awaited his touch, items that were intricate and highly detailed. They would require all of his training, but he would succeed. There was too much at stake for him not to.

Every waking hour, and many sleeping ones as well, was spent plotting out designs for the instruments he would need. There were moments he felt as if he was one of the great inventors from history, · like Thomas Edison creating the first light bulb. His inventions were not going to help brighten any dark rooms however, though the aid he would provide the citizens of Range City would most definitely use the light of justice to pierce the heart of darkness beating all too loudly these days.

He studied the design taped to the door of the machine shop—it too, was covered in notes and plans. Unlike the other areas however, the door was dedicated entirely to the design of a functional yet protective outfit. He wanted to incorporate some of his homemade arsenal into the uniform, but at the same time still have the flexibility to move around with ease.

The baking pan he'd been sanding down would eventually become an integral part of this uniform. Once he finished working and reinforcing the already sturdy metal, it would become a protective chest plate. He already had the design for the plate picked out, smiling at his creativeness.

The wall to the immediate right of the door held perhaps the most intricate and detailed blueprints. These were for something special he dreamed up; a weapon he could use to subdue any would-be criminals. This amazing piece of hardware would most definitely be the hardest of his creations to make, but it could very well be the most important. He also had a gut feeling this particular item would become his signature weapon; a pneumatic gun by design, but bullets would not be needed. No, that simply would not fit his theme. This gun would require a very special kind of ammo.

So much work left to do, he chastised himself for wasting time reflecting on his concepts. The law abiding citizens needed him. The crooks of Range City were getting too comfortable in their criminal ways, and yet here he was patting himself on the back for his own cleverness. This simply would not do. He would need to be ever vigilant in his work ethic if he was going to have any hope at all of succeeding. Time was too precious a commodity for him to waste spending on his pride.

He turned back to his work bench, and grabbed the sander. After putting the finishing touches on the smooth metal, he walked over to the heating element where the melted down steel could still be heard bubbling away. To add the final decorative shape he desired to the metal pan, he would have to heat it in order for the metal to become more pliable. It was tedious work, but the end result would be well worth the effort.

Needing to break up some of the monotony, Benji turned on the new stereo system he kept in the machine shop for entertainment. He twisted the tuning dial looking for some music he could work to. He thought briefly of putting in one of his Green Day CDs, but decided he would rather have the variety the local music channel, 105.7, would provide. Instead of hearing the electric sound of a guitar riff, the voice of a reporter caught his full attention.

"Residents of Range City woke up this morning to the disturbing news of an incredible bank robbery. The First National Bank was literally cleaned out sometime in the early morning hours. At this time, it is still unclear how the robber or robbers were able to enter the building, as nothing was caught on the surveillance tapes, and no security alarms were triggered. The police appear to have no viable leads, as evidence has yet to turn up. Police Chief Anderson had this to say."

Benji listened intently as he waited for the police chief's comments to be played. He did not have to wait long as the Chief's deep voice came rumbling out of the stereo's speakers.

"Seeing as this is now an official investigation, I cannot comment on what evidence we may or may not have found. I assure everyone, the person or persons responsible for this crime will be caught. Thank you, that is all."

The reporter jumped in, picking up right where he had left off. *"When hearing of the crime this morning, Mayor Martinez called a quick press conference, and released these statements."*

There was a slight pause before the determined yet tired voice of Range City's Mayor played. *"Good morning everyone. I am sure you all know by now the First National Bank was the target of a robbery sometime last night. I promise the good citizens of Range City that this office will not rest until the perpetrators of this dastardly crime are apprehended and brought to justice.*

I will provide the police department of our fair city with whatever resources they need to bring this investigation to a close. Thank you all for coming."

There was a few seconds of dead air before the reporter returned. *"This is another crime in a long list of incidents the Mayor has been forced to deal with since taking office. The crime rate has hit an all time high this year, culminating these past few weeks with the shooting death of Jimmy Davis, the young chef from Chez Louis Ristoranté, and now the robbery of the city's largest financial institution.*

I did have the opportunity to speak with bank manager, Ms. Jill Lee, about the robbery. When I asked Ms. Lee how robbers could have gotten away with the cash so easily, her comment was, 'Only some kind of evil genius could defeat our security system.' In other news…"

Benji reached over and flipped the stereo off. It had definitely not been the pick-me-up he was hoping to get from some good old loud music. Instead, what he got was another large dose of reality; the news of the robbery felt like a swift kick in the stomach, and he needed to sit down.

He could not believe what he had heard. The mentioning of Jimmy's death by the reporter had been another slap in his face as well. It was all so overwhelming that for the briefest of seconds he considered packing his bags and leaving the city to fend for itself. A shame came over him, and he could only offer up a disgusted shake of his head as an apology. He would not run with his tail tucked between his legs; that was a coward's way out, and he was no coward.

Upon reflection, this robbery felt somehow different. There was more to this story than the police knew, he was sure of it. This crime had an underlying sliminess to it; whoever had pulled it off had to be incredibly smart. The bank manager may have been more correct than she knew when she used the term evil genius.

With a new sense of resolve, Benji took up the chest plate he had been working on, and began heating it anew. Time was of the essence now, even moreso. He was determined not to let this happen again, at least not on his watch. With a sense of fierce determination, he turned his full attention to the task at hand.

Meanwhile across town, in his cushy secret lair, the Ice Cream Man was enjoying the spoils of his evil plotting. His plan had worked to perfection, his young minions followed their instructions to the letter, depositing their il-gotten booty here in his secret hideaway. They had of course returned to their homes none the wiser of participating in perhaps the greatest robbery ever.

It had almost been *too* easy. He could not wait until he would put his next evil plot into motion. Sitting atop a mound of bags filled with the citizens of Range City's hard earned money, enjoying a cup of tea, the Ice Cream Man cackled with glee.

CHAPTER 12

Crime Wave

For two weeks, Range City was ravaged as one major crime after another took place. First the bank, then the art museum, followed by the private residences of some of the city's wealthiest citizens. Each crime was similar in that not a trace of evidence was found.

The robberies took place under the noses of some of the best and most hi-tech security systems money could buy; the lack of leads had the police completely baffled. It was as if a ghost would float in, burglarize, and then simply vanish without a trace. With no witnesses and absolutely no trace evidence the official investigation into the crimes had come to a complete stand still.

The citizens were up in arms over the ordeal as well. It was bad enough their hometown had become a haven for the unlawful, but now high profile crimes were being committed with impunity. In their critical eyes, the police department was showing how inadequate they were to handle a crime spree of this kind, and the Mayor's office was showing itself to be utterly inept in trying to prevent any further damage from being done.

The eerie method of the most recent robberies was the talk of the town. Rumors and innuendo could be heard slipping from the whispering mouths of the ladies at the beauty salon, the veterans enjoying a cold beer at the American Legion, the patrons of the Wal-Mart, and even worried members of the city council. Everyone was wondering who or what would be hit next. One favorite topic of conversation was who the mastermind behind such ingeniously planned capers was. The *Range City Star Courier* carried front page stories with daily updates from the police department and Mayor's office. These updates were limited in their scope, so rumors were starting to surface that the FBI would soon be called in to help.

The police department's major crime decision was working around the clock to try and come up with any lead. Even the smallest or insignificant piece of evidence could be used to blow the case wide open, but as of yet not one shred had turned up. Police Chief Anderson could be found sitting at his desk into all hours of the night, poring over the case files, trying to find anything he could give to the townsfolk that might give them hope. Like every other officer in the department however, he kept coming up empty.

The Mayor was at an equal loss with how to proceed, and therefore was not fairing any better. The people were demanding action, and rightfully so. Under his watch the crime rate increased rapidly every year, and now with this new wave, the already tense concern they were feeling boiled over into a downright uproar. There were only so many resources for him to provide, though, and the police department already burnt up its overtime budget for the entire year trying to quell the overflow of criminal activity. These new crimes needed top priority, and would only make the city's financial dilemma even worse. Mayor Martinez knew it was only a matter of time before another burglary would take place, but what could he do to prevent it than he was already doing? He felt like he was drowning, with no one around to toss him a life preserver.

Little did the people of Range City know the perpetrator behind this wicked spree was also the same person making regular passes through their neighborhoods, selling tasty frozen treats to their children. Treats which in turn became the means to gain control of the city's youth, giving the villainous Ice Cream Man the necessary gang to pull off such seemingly impossible and dastardly deeds.

Upon arriving in and researching Range City, the Ice Cream Man had discovered the remnants of an ancient nickel mine. Many of the old tunnels were closed from cave-ins, but others were still accessible if one knew where to look. From these long forgotten tunnels someone with the intelligence of the evil genius variety could gain access to the entire city's water and sewer system, and from there move virtually undetected to any building, whether it be a business or private residence, within city limits. Of course with his superior intellect, the Ice Cream Man knew how to defeat the most sophisticated of security systems; he had managed to escape from a top secret military installation, after all. He passed this knowledge on to his minions through the secret message filled music he played while driving his routes.

No one—not the police, nor the Mayor or city council, nor the citizens themselves—suspected for one second the perfect crimes of the recent spree were in fact being committed by their very own children. With the controlling influence of someone so evil, the children moved wraith-like through their intended targets with no one the wiser. When they woke up the next morning, they themselves had no idea what they had done. All they knew was they were unusually tired, and for some odd reason, sometimes they did not smell too good.

While the officials of Range City scurried around like insects trying to figure out how such burglaries could be happening, the Ice Cream Man was sitting back, enjoying a good laugh at their futility. Reading the local newspaper each morning had become his favorite pastime, well, maybe his second favorite. His first was throwing large sums of money on the floor of his laboratory, and rolling around on it. Soon—very soon—he would have a new batch of stolen loot to frolic in.

Unbeknownst to the Ice Cream Man, another citizen of Range City was also hard at work putting the finishing touches on his own secret plans. His was not a scheme to rob citizens of their cherished belongings, but it was a means to bring justice to Range City, and a way to put a stop to the nightmares the city could not seem to wake from. Benjamin "Benji" Winters, former army captain and head chef of a gourmet restaurant, was almost ready to answer destiny's call.

CHAPTER 13

Dressed for Success

In the twilight hours, with the sun turning a beautiful shade of dark red as it began to set for its evening rest, Benji put the finishing touches on the last of his projects. Over the past couple of weeks, while the new wave of crime was holding Range City hostage, he had worked nearly nonstop on what would become the many tools and gadgets of his arsenal. Tonight had been dedicated solely to the completion of the uniform, which would offer some protection and hide his true identity lest he find himself behind bars, instead of the criminals who rightfully belonged there.

When he first set out on this odyssey, he was not exactly sure what kind of uniform he would require. Originally, he figured he would venture out in a pair of his old army fatigues and possibly a dark ski mask. On further thought, he decided he needed to move in an entirely separate direction, or he more than likely would have been wrongfully accused of being one of the crooks he was trying to capture. In the end he decided he needed something to set himself apart.

After giving some thought to what he might wear, he realized a simple outfit would never do. If he was going to be a true hero and champion, then he needed to be known for more than just his actions. He would have to become a symbol the people of Range City could rally around. He would need to have flair and panache, and the uniform he wore would have to reflect that attitude. The vision he'd experienced while lying unconscious in the hospital showed how both aspects of his life could play a part in trying to save the city. A melding of the knowledge and experience he gained from being in the army, and also his training in the culinary arts, was what would be required to complete his transformation. It only made sense that the costume, for lack of a better word, would follow the same pattern.

Benji knew exactly what kind of costume he should create. A combining of his skills would result in a military style uniform with some added bonuses. The look of the outfit would grant him the icon status he would need to drive fear into the hearts of all evil doers. Only then would he truly become the hero he envisioned, and one the residents of Range City could be proud of.

When he was discharged from his military service, Benji had the foresight to keep everything the army had given him. He packed it all up, and brought it with him to his new home where it had sat somewhat forgotten until now. The bags containing his military gear contained mostly old camouflage uniforms of various colors and designs. There was also some of his old gear; heavy nylon climbing rope, his old helmet, a favorite backpack, along with many other odds and ends of varying degrees of importance. Those bags had found their way into the machine shop alongside the kitchen implements, ready to offer up their own contributions to the cause.

After rifling through the old duffel bags looking for the uniforms, he settled on a pair of pants designed with the colors for urban camouflage and containing several large pockets. The gray, white, and black swirls with a hint of blue were perfect for what he had in mind. Also, the black combat boots, though in desperate need of a good polishing, were exactly what this type of work called for. Lastly, he pulled out his old battered helmet.

It was funny, but the head gear always reminded him of a shrunken samurai helmet. He felt this was an appropriate comparison, as the samurai warriors lived their lives based on a code of honor. He would try his best to live up to their example, as he too, was trying to do the honorable thing by serving as the self-appointed protector of the innocent. His helmet needed some work, though, as it would have to be strengthened and some key adjustments made.

From the bag of pots and pans he took from the restaurant, he selected several of the baking and cooking sheets. At one time these pans were used to bake delicious desserts for the patrons of Chez Louis' Ristoranté. Now they would serve a much grander purpose as protective armor, though they would need to be shaped and reinforced. The end result would be a magnificent sight to behold.

There were a few items he had to acquire on his own that would become important elements of his costume as well. These included a utility tool belt. He tweaked the belt somewhat to meet his needs, but little else had to be done to it. Another key component was a bullet-proof Kevlar vest. He had to call in a favor from one of his old army buddies, who as luck would have it, happened to be a supply sergeant. That sure made it easier to obtain, not having to cut through all the bureaucratic red tape.

Creating his costume reminded Benji of baking his famous chocolate mousse. He now had the ingredients required, and all that was left was to mix everything together to create one glorious masterpiece. And that was what he had done.

Everything was as ready as he could make it. All pieces of the costume were fitted and polished to a gleaming sheen. All alterations were made, as well as any needed repairs. The moment of truth had finally arrived. If the old axiom was correct and clothes really did make the man, then the crooks of Range City better beware—this costume made him a hero.

He felt a little foolish standing alone in the machine shop in his boxer shorts and socks, but the embarrassment soon faded. As he began getting dressed, a realization settled over him; he understood and—more importantly, accepted—after this evening his life would be forever altered. On some levels, he would cease to be Benjamin Winters, mild mannered chef, and would take on an altogether new persona. Instead of being gold old Benji, he would become like the knights of old and be a paladin for the side of good.

He thought briefly of Jimmy. His young friend had challenged that someone needed to do something about what was happening to their city. Well, Benji was taking up the challenge and doing something about it tonight. He was on the verge of fulfilling his vow to the young chef who had become his best friend. It was an emotional moment, and he reached up and wiped a tear from his eye as the memory of his friend played itself out.

He took a deep breath to help calm his nerves, looking at all of the items he created, taking a moment to inventory them. The moment was close to perfect.

Without any further ado, he began changing into the costume that would now define his purpose in life. "It's go time," he said out loud beginning to get himself psyched up.

He put on a long sleeved warm-up shirt which he slipped over his head with ease. Next, came the urban camouflage pants, which he pulled up over the shirt tail, securing them around his waist. The legs were a little baggy, but they were supposed to be that way. The two pockets located slightly above the knees on the side of each leg only added to the effect. The legs did taper down to his ankle, and he folded each hem to make it easier for each pant leg to be tucked into the boots.

The recently-polished combat boots shone in the light of the machine shop, any soldier would be envious of the shine Benji was able to bring out of his old boots. With the dinginess of age now gone, they looked like they could be sitting in a shoe store, brand new. He slipped the comfortable and durable boots on, taking his time lacing them up, making sure he did not miss a notch. He stood, feeling better than he had in a long, long time.

His excitement was rising steadily with each new article of clothing he put on. He felt invincible, and took this as a good sign. Still feeling invigorated, he grabbed his homemade shin guards, formerly known as two large cookie pans, and latched them around each leg. They resembled the guards uses by major league baseball catchers, only a little slimmer, shorter, and streamlined. The metal of the shin guards, like all the metal of this costume, was reinforced with the stainless steel he had melted down. Several coats of the liquid steel had been applied, making the shin guards and other items incredibly durable and nearly impenetrable. The metal was also polished to a high sheen, causing it to sparkle brightly like a precious gem when caught just right by the light.

The most important piece of the ensemble came next, the most complicated, the one he was most proud of. The elaborate chest and back plates were a work of engineering art, a true masterpiece. This portion of the body armor was the true melding of both aspects of his life, and it was a thing of absolute technical beauty—a marvel any industrial engineer who was lucky enough to behold it would be left envious and in awe. The actual armor opened similar to an oyster shell, which he could then pull over his head. It covered his entire chest and stomach area as well as his shoulders and back, with clips located under his armpits, at his ribcage and then again at his waist, slightly covering the waistline of his pants. Once locked into place, it was completely secure. Benji had taken the Kevlar vest and modified it so the reinforced stainless steel of the chest and back plates fit over the vest. The bulletproof material actually became the lining of the armor.

Once he slipped the body armor on, and slid the clips until they were locked, he was pleased with how evenly the weight was distributed; comfortable and allowing for his full range of motion. This was important, he was sure things would get physical once he engaged the criminals of Range City. He also needed a certain degree of flexibility to utilize the various weapons he had at his disposal.

The metal had come from different pans coated with the steel. The front and back plates were fashioned after the Roman praetorian guard armor in that the chest design was of the pectoral and abdominal muscles of a well developed man, while the back followed the natural contours of the human body. The effect was nearly perfect. In the center of the chest plate at the area covering his heart, Benji added the circular bottom of a large stewing pot for extra protection.

Over the metal of the back plate, hung a black modified backpack. The straps which normally would go over the wearer's shoulders were slid through small slits cut in the metal, and were

THE ADVENTURES OF CAPTAIN KITCHEN

clipped to the inside lining, holding the pack securely in place. Benji also added small hooks in the back plate for the bag to hang on for stability and to distribute some of the weight of the contents more evenly.

Directly under the left shoulder area next to the backpack was a black leather holster. It hung all the way down the back plate ending just above the waist. A polished wood handle with black rubber tubing disappearing into the top of the backpack. This was his greatest accomplishment: the pneumatic plastic wrap blaster. This rifle was his great equalizer in the fight against crime.

The final touch to the body armor was a blue apron, fashioned like a cape, covering the backpack. This had been his favorite apron back when he was just a chef. The dark blue color matched the azure hue of the urban camouflage. Though not a seamstress, he was rather proud of himself for the way he was able to rework the stitching of the apron, and have it attached to the lining of the back plate at each shoulder. The cape was a cheesy touch to the costume, but he liked it nevertheless.

With the body armor securely in place, he moved on to the next items. Over his arms, he slid two finely crafted metal bracers. They were attached to fingerless gloves like those one might see ultimate fighters wear. The bracers covered his forearms from the elbow all the way to the back of each hand. They fit snugly on each arm, and included a small hinge allowing the wrists to to bend normally. They also carried a surprise; a spring loaded projectile located on the top of each arm. To activate the firing mechanism he need only bend his wrist all the way down and make a tight fist. The right bracer contained a butter knife attached to a small coil of rope, while the left held a large serving spoon loaded with pepper.

The icing on the cake was the final touch to the costume. The once drab green army commando helmet was now a shining head gear rivaling the greatest of medieval helms. A Knight of the Round Table would have been proud to call it their own. The helmet was coated in the silver steel, and gleamed like a diamond. The face plate was in the style of a Corinthian helmet, showing his eyes but with a piece of metal hanging between, covering his nose, and two pieces of metal tapered down to points to cover each cheek, with a slim rectangular gap running down the middle. The helmet fitted to his head tightly, and could be strapped under the chin for added security.

But before slipping his helmet on, Benji rubbed black shoe polish around his face, and pulled a thin black mask over his head, similar to the fireproof hoods race car drivers wear, covering his entire head, with an open area from forehead to chin. The rest of the mask was tucked beneath the shirt collar covering the throat area.

With a final deep breath to steel his resolve, Benji took the helmet from its place on the work bench, and with reverence, slipped it on his head. After locking the chin strap in place, he reached up with both hands to make sure it was centered. There were still a few items he needed to put on, like the tool belt-holsters containing his frying pan clubs, and the thigh bandolier holding the sharpened throwing forks, but for all intents and purposes he was ready.

When he finished adding the assorted items of his arsenal, Benji walked out of the machine shop, and breathed in the crisp, fresh air of early evening. Tonight would be the culmination of a journey he had been thrust upon since Jimmy's passing. He felt completely energized by what he was about to do, and paused to reflect on the deeper meaning of what he was committing himself to. In his heart he knew it was the right thing.

"This is for you Jimmy," he whispered staring up at the calm night sky.

With a nod of his head for assurance, he walked over to the garage and pushed the heavy wooden door up, revealing the Harley Davidson Sportster parked inside. Not wanting to hesitate any longer than he already had, he climbed aboard the motorcycle and fired it up. The loud rumble of a finely tuned engine filled the interior of the garage as he slowly backed outside, and turned it around so he was facing the road that would take him out to the highway, and from there, into Range City.

With a last glance over his equipment, he throttled the Harley up, speeding off to begin his one man assault against the criminals of Range City.

Chapter 14

A Hero is Born

The motorcycle engine purred contentedly, and the countryside zoomed past at a blur as the self-appointed champion of Range City sped along. making his way into town. The rush of wind was a welcome side effect, as the evening was humid, and Benji was sweating freely under his costume.

Even though the temperature was high for this time of night, he thought it more likely the perspiration covering his body was the result of the nervous excitement he was feeling. Tonight was the night everything would come together; the criminals, crooks, and wannabe hoods of Range City better look out because tonight he would be on the prowl. He would be the lifeguard watching out and protecting the innocent.

He knew this scheme of his was incredibly far-fetched, like something out of a Marvel comic book. Even though he did not have super powers like the heroes of those books, he was not powerless. He had the vision and the drive to do what was right. Those traits had brought him this far, and he was sure they would not fail him. Tonight was merely the first step in a much larger and far greater journey.

A green road sign came into view as he steered the bike down the country highway. He smiled with increasing excitement as he passed it by. Range City was only five miles away. He throttled the Harley up even faster knowing he was so close; over the next hill he was able to make out the lights of Range City. Finally, it was time, time to do some good.

Benji passed the large sign welcoming all visitors to the city, knowing that after another mile he would find himself smack in the middle of downtown Range City. Herein lay a new dilemma; with his costume on, he would stick out like a sore thumb. He needed to remain incognito for as long as possible to achieve the desired success. The element of surprise was a valuable tool, perhaps prove to be even more valuable than any of his own inventions.

Due to the hour, traffic was light, and so far his odd appearance had gone unnoticed by what drivers he did pass. He would need to get out of sight quickly however, it was only a matter of time before he was spotted. His plan was to park and stash the motorcycle someplace easily accessible, in case he needed to make a quick getaway. The most appropriate place to do that was in the alley behind the local library. It was rarely used, and gave him a straight shot onto the main street heading out of town.

He coasted into the alley, killing the engine as he entered. Still straddling the large bike, he walked it in a tight circle so the bike was facing out the same way he had entered. Stepping off, he looked around the empty alley. The night was so still, the air heavy with humidity, more than likely signaling an impending storm. He was ready for action, no matter what the climate.

As he'd worked on his tools and costume, he had listened faithfully to his police scanner. Doing so, he'd learned there was a series of convenience store robberies, and that the police seemed to believe all of these hold-ups were the work of the same group of three individuals. This was where he decided to make his first stand, with these relatively small crimes as compared to the major activity going on throughout the city. It would give him a chance to field test his equipment. It would also be a good time to test his own physical abilities.

His next step was to gain a high vantage point. The street the library was on was also home to three separate convenient stores, all located within two blocks. None of these stores had fallen prey to the robbers as of yet, which made them likely targets. With that in mind, Benji made his way to the roof of a neighboring building, where he would be able to see all three stores.

The building was two stories, holding a family-owned auto supplies store. There was easy access to the roof via a set of stairs leading from the backdoor of the actual shop, to the business offices on the second floor. By standing on the wooden railing of the second floor landing, he was able to pull himself up onto the roof. After crossing the few feet to the front of the building, he had a perfect view of the three convenience stores, and directly across the street was a streetlamp hanging over the road, which would provide his means of quick descent if the situation called for it. All he could do now was wait, and let fate deal its hand.

Time dragged as first an hour and then a second went by. All of the other businesses had closed up shop for the night, leaving the convenience stores to become an oasis for those needing gas or a late night snack.

He was on the verge of calling it a night when he caught movement out of the corner of his eye; someone was crossing the street at a brisk pace, coming from farther down the street where it was dark with shadows. There was a low grating sound, as if heavy metal was being dragged slowly across concrete. Benji watched with curiosity as a young kid, maybe twelve or thirteen, joined another child of relatively the same age standing before an open hole in the street. This was obviously the source of the noise he heard earlier, as somehow the first kid had managed to pry up and move a manhole cover. His curiosity deepened as the two minors disappeared down the hole to the nether regions of Range City, followed by the same low grating sound as the manhole cover was slid back into place.

He barely had time to register what had taken place when a loud commotion coming from the direction of the convenience stores drew his focus back to the other end and side of the street. Three men were exiting the convenient store, all younger, probably in their early twenties, and he could clearly see one was carrying a large handgun. The strange incident with the two younger children now forgotten, he gave his equipment a quick once over. This was it, the moment of truth. These three crooks had committed a crime, and it was his job to thwart their getaway.

It was time to go to work.

He stared out at the streetlight gauging the distance in his head. Raising his right arm to shoulder level, he took a deep calming breath, aimed, and fired. There was a slight jolt of recoil and a swooshing sound as the knife with the rope attached to it shot out from the metal bracer and flew through the night. His aim was true, and the knife looped around the streetlight several times before losing momentum and stopping. He gave the rope a hard tug making sure it was set, and would not unleash itself. Satisfied the rope was secure enough to hold his weight, Benji climbed on the lip of the roof, grabbed hold of the rope with both hands, and swung himself down to street level.

He felt like Tarzan, swinging through the jungle on a vine, as he touched down on the concrete of the sidewalk beside the streetlight. He almost let out a primal yell, but remembering the importance of surprise, he held back, and began sprinting towards the trio of crooks. The excitement of the moment continued to build with each step, and he felt like he might burst at the seams. He was only a block away from the store when he landed from his swing so he closed the gap relatively quickly.

The three robbers were laughing, celebrating their conquest, as they walked casually to their getaway vehicle. They were so nonchalant with their actions, as if they did not have a care in the world. Crime had become so prevalent in Range City, and they had gotten away with robbing stores so many times, they seemed completely confidant they would walk away scott free this time as well. Benji smiled, thinking how wrong they were, and what a surprise they were in for.

"What the heck is that?" one of the crooks asked, as Benji entered the store's parking lot. All three robbers were staring, open-mouthed, at him. With the neon lights of the store glaring off his body armor, he must be a sight. The element of surprise worked to perfection, the robbers were motionless with shock. He took several more steps closer until he was only a few feet from two of the three young robbers standing by their car. Two were on the driver side, including the guy with the gun, while the remaining crook was standing next to the passenger's side door.

"Step away from the vehicle," he ordered loudly.

"Man, you must be outta your mind. What'd you think this is, Halloween?" the guy standing next to the passenger door said, stepping back slowly, and reaching into his pocket.

Benji saw the young man's arm move, and understood what the motion was signaling. The others remained rooted to their spots, unsure of what their next move should be. Raising his left arm, and pointing it, fist down, at the leader he warned, "I wouldn't do that if I were you."

"Yeah, well you aren't me, fool." The young crook pulled out a 9mm automatic, but before he could bring it to bear, Benji triggered the firing mechanism in his bracer. The spoon filled with pepper flew true as it struck the dumbfounded robber right between the eyes, spilling the pepper down his face, finding its way into the perp's eyes, causing them to sting mercilessly and begin to water. It also shot up his nose as he sucked in a breath, causing a sneezing fit. As he wiped at his eyes, the gun dropped to the ground, momentarily forgotten.

"Gesundheit," Benji said sarcastically.

The other crook, seeing what had befallen his comrade, though still confused by Benji's strange appearance, finally remembered he was able to move and dove to the pavement intent on snatching up the handgun in order to defend himself.

Benji knew what he had in mind, and without hesitating, reached down to his right thigh, where the sharpened three pronged forks were sheathed. In his rush, he managed to grab three. Taking only seconds to aim at his intended target, he threw the forks with uncanny accuracy.

The one-time salad forks flew arrow straight. The first hit the pavement and the handgun at the same time, causing it to scoot even further out of reach. The other two utensil missiles found new homes in the back of the robber's hand and just under the elbow. The satisfying yelp of pain was music to Benji's ears.

"Well I've already stuck a fork in you, two actually, so I'd say you're done."

Seeing his partners in crime being so treated, the third robber decided to abandon them. Fumbling with the keys in his hand, the robber was unable to get the car door open, and so instead took off running down the street.

Benji jogged around what would have been the getaway car so he had a clear line of fire. He reached back with his right hand, and unzipped a side pouch. From there he pulled out his version of a bola, made from three heavy whisks and tough nylon rope, which he twirled over his head It began making a loud whirring sound as it picked up speed; as it seemed to hit a crescendo, he sent it flying in pursuit of the fleeing crook.

The spinning whisk and rope contraption caught the unsuspecting crook around the knees, entangling itself like a boa constrictor. He fell face-first onto the concrete of the road, smashing his nose with a sickening crunching sound. He rolled onto his back, semiconscious, a steady stream of blood dribbling from his broken nose.

Benji followed his throw, and soon found himself standing over the dazed criminal. From out of one of the large pockets, he took two large, plastic zip ties. He kicked the crook back over onto his stomach, and secured the plastic ties in a figure eight, locking the robber's hands in makeshift handcuffs. "Well, now the garbage is tied up, I guess I can finish taking out the trash."

The first robber, who had finally wiped enough pepper out of his eyes and was able to see again, charged after Benji, trying to catch him off guard. Hearing the footsteps of his rapidly approaching attacker, Benji spun with cat-like reflexes, and removed two medium sized pot lids from the bottom pouch of the backpack. The lids were smoothed down, the edges dulled with a heavy coat of the stainless steel, basically making them flying cudgels. He threw the lids like a Frisbee, with as much force as he could muster. The first lid caught the robber in the midsection, stopping him in his tracks and doubling him over at the waist. The other lid smacked him right on the top of his bent head, and he teetered for a second, then toppled over lying in the middle of the street, unmoving.

By this time, the convenience store clerk, still shook up from the initial robbery, had run outside to see what the commotion was about. Seeing Benji standing in the street in all of his body armored glory had turned the clerk into a statue, frozen with shock.

The second robber, still yelping in pain from the two forks sticking out of his arm, got to his feet, and moved towards the confused clerk. Seeing this, realizing he was going to use the clerk as a human shield, Benji decided it was time for his secret weapon.

"It's time to wrap things up," he said loudly, as he moved within a few feet of the cowardly robber. He reached over his left shoulder, and removed the pneumatic rifle from its resting place in the leather holster. Holding the gun with both hands at waist level, he flipped a switch with his thumb, and fired.

Powered by a large CO_2 canister, a long steady stream of plastic wrap came blasting out. A rustling sound filled the night as the plastic wrap made its way across the parking lot, until the wrap hit the frightened crook in the chest, adhering itself tightly, wrapping around his upper body. The crook yipped like a scared dog as he was quickly overcome by the plastic.

Benji moved the gun up and down until the crook was covered from neck to ankles in the plastic wrap. He released the trigger and the wrap was cut. The crook looked like a ridiculous imitation of a plastic mummy.

The clerk, so startled by the strange turn of events, reached out to touch the crook which caused him to fall over. The clerk looked at Benji in complete amazement. "Uh... thank you?"

"No problem," Benji replied proudly. "You might want to call the police."

"I already did."

Off in the distance sirens could be heard approaching. The whole incident had lasted a few minutes, yet to Benji it felt as if time had stopped completely. With the police on their way, he knew he better make his exit. "I think my work here is done." He turned to make his way back to the awaiting motorcycle.

"Wait a minute," the store clerk called from behind him. "Who are you?"

Benji turned and stared at the young clerk, not really sure how to respond.

"A friend," he replied, before running back to the alley. The sound of the Harley soon reverberated through the night as he sped away.

CHAPTER 15

Successes & Schemes

After vanquishing the three thugs, Benji returned to the motorcycle, and made his way back home. The absolute euphoria of actually being able to thwart a crime was indescribable. It had all happened so fast, almost as if he had dreamed the whole experience. It was real though, his bubbling excitement reassured him of that. This evening had been a raging success, and he could not contain his jubilation any longer.

"Woo-hoo!" Benji's shout of victory echoed loudly across the otherwise peaceful countryside.

The rush of adrenaline from the fight with the robbers had yet to subside. He still felt like he would burst with pride of what he accomplished. Tonight he had stopped one minor crime. Who knew what tomorrow might bring? He couldn't wait to find out. He gave thought to returning to the city to see if he could find any more action, but dismissed the notion quickly. He did not want to push his luck; he barely got away from the scene ahead of the police.

Still, he wanted to celebrate the success of a mission accomplished. Beating those lowly crooks was the culmination of a lot of hard work, and now he wanted to revel in the moment. Victory was a sensation he could definitely get used to, it felt so good to actually be doing something constructive. He was part of the solution now, and hopefully it would not be long before word spread throughout the criminal underground.

The only downside was so many of his weapons had to be left behind, something he had not foreseen. Everything would have to be replaced of course, but now he knew they would work so it wouldn't be a problem. He still had plenty of equipment left over from his excursion to the restaurant, and what he did not have, could always be ordered. This was definitely something he would have to give more thought to, as he planned on becoming a lot more active. He would need to have ready replacements on hand, but for now he could get by with what he had.

With the excitement of the evening finally starting to wane, he began to feel tired. The heightened level his senses reached during the night's activities was beginning to take their toll. He actually had to stifle a yawn where mere minutes before he wanted to charge headlong, back into the fray.

Benji slipped out of his costume as quickly as he could, until he was left standing in his Sponge Bob Squarepants boxer shorts. He replaced each item in the machine shop so they would be ready for tomorrow. There was something else he would have to perfect as well; he could not wander back and forth between the shop and the house in just his under shorts. He would simply have to come up with a better system, one more item to add to the growing list of things to do. Yes, tonight had been a rousing success, a blow struck for the side of justice, but there was still much more work in need of being done.

Giving in to the growing exhaustion settling over his body, Benji walked the short distance to the old farm house, made his way to the already darkened bedroom, and collapsed onto his large four poster bed. Being a hero was a tiring business. He chuckled softly at his joke as he drifted off to the best night of sleep he had experienced in a long, long time. This time his dreams were not nightmares filled with images of criminals run amok or even more frightening, of Jimmy being shot. They were full of more pleasant scenes of his new brand of justice being doled out to the betterment of Range City.

In a secret laboratory on the opposite side of the city, a different celebration of sorts was taking place. The villainous Ice Cream Man was reveling in his most recent success, the robbery of the Range City First Federal Savings and Loan bank. The bags of money his minions brought him were piled in the corner, joining the loot and spoils from his other magnificently planned conquests.

Things could not have gone any better. It was like taking candy from a baby. With his brilliant and equally evil genius level IQ he was more than a match for the foolishly inept police, so how could he have thought otherwise?

With the rash of high profile robberies he and his minions had pulled off, he now controlled the cash flow of the city. All the other financial institutions in the city were quaking in their proverbial boots, knowing it was a matter of time before they too, would fall victim to his evil whims, and in good time they might. He had bigger fish to fry however.

With his young lackeys slipping in and out of the city's most secure facilities at his will, he knew the town was basically being held hostage. He had the financial power to get whatever his heart desired, but it was not enough. To truly take over and hold all the power, he would have to eliminate one man. If he could take out the one person who was the symbol of control and assurance, then Range City would be his.

It was time to put the next phase of his scheme into play.

The kidnapping of Mayor Martinez would be the shining 24 carat diamond in his crown jewels of crime. Once he had control of the Mayor, all else would fall into place, and with Range City as his power base, there would be no stopping him. Oh, if those fools at the military installation could only see him now. They would rue the day they used him as their pet guinea pig.

First thing first however, the Mayor would have to be removed. This would take some extra planning if he wanted things to go off without a hitch. He would need some new recruits for this extra special mission, he might even need to make an appearance himself. It was time this stagnant waste of a city knew who the mastermind behind the recent wave of perfect crime was.

As the moon began to descend in the predawn sky, the evil Ice Cream Man decided it was time to sleep, even evil geniuses need to rest, after all. He had a long day ahead, scouting out the perfect recruits for this most important of capers. It would not do if he was not at his evil best.

The latest batch of special frozen treats was ready to be distributed to the chosen few who would make up his elite kidnapping force, all he needed to do was choose wisely. It was only a matter of time before Range City would find out who their true master was. He, the dreaded Ice Cream Man, would rule this city and then the world!

With visions of upcoming successes still lingering, he slipped off to his sleeping chamber, completely secure in the knowledge there was no one out there who could stop him.

CHAPTER 16

The Morning After

Benji woke early the next morning feeling completely refreshed. His muscles were a bit sore, but nothing he could not banish with a few minor stretching exercises. The sun was peeking through the heavy drapes pulled together over the bedroom window, and he was surprised to see it was only 8:00 a.m. It felt much later; he had only been sleeping a few short hours, but he felt better than he had for quite some time.

Anxious to see if there was any news about the exploits the night before, he got out of bed, worked out the kinks in his muscles, and hopped into the shower. The steaming hot water pelting his skin worked out the last remnants of tightness in his body. Rushing through the rest of his morning ritual, he then grabbed his truck keys, and headed for the city.

One drawback of living in a rural area was he did not receive his newspaper until the afternoon, and he simply could not wait that long. He was as excited as a kid at their own birthday party, dying to tear into the first present. He decided to have breakfast at his favorite truck stop diner, where he could get the early edition of the paper, and hopefully read about his exploits over a big plate of bacon and eggs.

The 18 Wheeler was located right inside the city limits, next to the on ramp for Interstate 80. It was a regular haunt for truck drivers making their way across the country, and the very definition of a greasy spoon. The coffee was strong and hot, and their breakfast was the best in town. As a chef, he knew good food when he ate it, and The 18 Wheeler's eggs were better than his own.

As he pulled into the parking lot, he spied the object of his desire. Right next to the diner's entrance were three small metal vending machines, each holding a different newspaper. Of the three, Benji was only interested in the middle one, as it held the local paper - the Range City Star Courier.

He half-walked and half-jogged across the parking lot, digging in his jeans pocket for the coins he would need to purchase the paper. Nearly out of breath from his excitement, he finally found himself standing in front of the newspaper machine, dropping the three coins into the awaiting slot, one after the other. Benji reached out, grasped the handle located near the top, and pulled it down, careful to avert his eyes as he did not want to see the headlines just yet. He wanted to wait until he was inside the diner, sitting comfortably and sipping coffee, before he allowed himself to read the headlines. He wanted the moment to be perfect, and with that in mind, he rolled his edition of the Range City Star Courier up until it resembled small club, and entered the restaurant.

The place was as busy as it usually was this time of day. The hustle and bustle of activity along with the familiar sounds of clattering dishes and idle chatter sent a pang of longing through his gut. He had not given much thought to his time at Chez Louis' Ristoranté the last few weeks, what with being so busy with his preparations, but with this all too familiar atmosphere permeating his senses, he realized how much he missed the restaurant scene. He took a deep breath to squelch the growing lump of emotion trying to find a home in his throat. He had a new chosen profession now. It would do him no good to linger in the past.

The 18 Wheeler was a seat yourself kind of joint, and after looking over the lay of the land he spotted an empty booth off to his left. After making his way through the crowd, he slipped into a red booth with the comforting sound of well worn, well aged vinyl creaking as he settled his weight. He put the newspaper down on the table, and it began to unroll, so he pushed it farther away so he would be unable to see the front page. A pretty, middle-aged waitress hurried over and took his order. He ordered the same thing he always ordered, the number two breakfast platter, consisting of two eggs over medium, three strips of crispy bacon, and a side order of wheat toast. To round out his breakfast, he ordered a cup of coffee. It would be served black, but he would add his requisite two creams and two sugars once it arrived at his table.

The waitress returned rather quickly, coffee pot in hand. With a friendly wink, she reached over, flipped the cup on his table upright, and filled it. Benji doctored the coffee the way he liked it, and took a small sip. The mocha colored liquid was scalding hot, and it burnt his lip, causing him to jump back. He nearly spilled the rest of the mug into his lap. Relaxing once again, he took a more careful sip; this time the coffee went down smoothly. The flavor was perfect.

While waiting for his food to arrive, he sat back and tried to listen in on the conversations going on around him, hoping to overhear some snippet of gossip concerning his apprehension of the robbers the previous evening. He did manage to pick up something about a robbery, but the details were lost in the din of the background noise of the busy diner. There was a little bit of a let down as he could not hear anything that might be related to his heroics.

Along with a wide variety of clientele, The 18 Wheeler was also known for its above-standard service, and they did not disappoint this morning when only minutes later his food was brought to his table. The food smelled fabulous, and in response, his stomach growled loudly. He did not realize how hungry he was until the food was actually sitting in front of him.

Once he'd devoured an entire egg and swallowed the second piece of bacon, he took a long sip of his coffee, leaning back somewhat sated. The newspaper now held his full attention. He could not contain his curiosity any longer so he grabbed the newspaper, and flipped it over so he could see the headline.

Master Criminal Strikes Again—First Federal Savings & Loan Robbed

This was not the headline he was hoping to see, and a small wave of disappointment washed over him. He was not a vain man, but he had hoped with all the hard work he'd put into last night's success, someone would have noticed. He did feel ashamed however, thinking about his wounded pride when another major crime had taken place that would affect dozens of Range City citizens. Some hero he was turning out to be.

There was something familiar about the name of the bank he could not quite put his finger on. He scanned the article until his eyes came to rest on the address. The Range City First Federal Savings and Loan was located on the same street as the auto parts store he'd stationed himself on, and the store where his altercation had taken place. The bank had been robbed quite literally right under his nose.

The article did not give a time when the robbery was thought to have occurred. This meant it could have happened before he had arrived, or possibly after he had fled. That did not make sense though, as the police had shown up at the convenience store within minutes of his leaving, and he seriously doubted the robbery would have gone down with the police right there. The way these robberies were happening however, anything seemed possible.

He took another couple of bites of his rapidly cooling eggs, and tried to think back if anything out of the ordinary had occurred. The only thing he could remember that had seemed odd and out of place was the appearance of the two kids, and how they'd disappeared down the manhole to what he presumed were the sewers. It seemed highly unlikely that two young teens could be involved in such a seemingly impossible crime. It was more likely they had broken curfew, and were looking for a short cut home before being caught. The city's sewers seemed an odd choice for a short cut, though.

He took another long sip from his cup of coffee, and flipped the paper so he could check out the story under the fold. He was taken completely by surprise when he saw the headline. He smiled proudly as the big bold block letters announced, *Costumed Vigilante Captures Convenience Store Crooks.*

He looked up from the paper and knew he had a big goofy grin plastered all over his face. If he was not careful, he might give himself away. He gazed around the diner to see if anyone noticed his odd behavior, but thankfully everyone seemed to be minding their own business. Trying to rein in his exuberance, he read on.

"Does Range City have its own superhero? Well according to local convenience store cashier, Bobby Willis, the answer is yes. When three men arrived, men Range City police now believe to be responsible for a series of similar robberies, and attempted to rob Mr. Willis' place of employment, a costumed vigilante arrived in time to save the day. Using what Mr. Willis described as a mix of kitchen utensils and weapons, the vigilante was able to not only thwart the robbery, but was also able to detain the crooks until the authorities arrived."

The article went on, detailing his exploits using the young cashier's eyewitness account as the backbone of the story. The last couple lines of the article were what made him feel the best, like he was not alone in his opinion that Range City was in deep trouble.

"Does Range City have a superhero of its own? In this reporter's humble opinion I can only say I hope so! This city needs all the help it can get, and if there is someone out there, vigilante or not, who is willing to stand up and do something about the crime infesting this city, then more power to him. Mr. Willis commented that when asked who the costumed stranger was, the only reply he received was 'A friend'. Well let us all hope this person is a friend and more than that, let's hope this person is a hero."

The last paragraph summed up his own feelings perfectly. He checked the byline of the article so he would know the reporter's name. Spotting it, he committed the name Brooks Quinlan to memory. If this Brooks Quinlan shared his feelings on the subject of crime overrunning Range City, he could be an ally. He would have to give consideration to reaching out to Mr. Brooks as the reporter could prove to be a valuable resource.

He re-read the article before finishing his breakfast. He got up to leave, and went to grab the newspaper before thinking better of it. He left the money for his tab along with a healthy tip on the table next to the paper, the article about his exploits sitting face-up. Seeing the headline again made him smile anew.

He walked out of The 18 Wheeler and took in a deep breath of fresh air; somehow everything seemed cleaner crisper as if brand new. He felt so alive. He took one last look around at the city before heading back to his truck. He needed to get home, he had plenty of work to do before this evening's adventure. He wanted to prove the reporter, Quinlan, right. He was a friend to the city and so much more. He was the hero Range City longed for.

CHAPTER 17

Captain Kitchen!

The next week went by following much the same pattern. Benji would venture out at night, usually after 10 p.m., fight crime, and be back to the farmhouse between 2-3 a.m. He would catch a few hours of sleep, and then head back into the city to read about his late night forays in the early edition of the *Range City Star Courier.* The same reporter, Brooks Quinlan, covered every story, and was rapidly gaining a following.

During his "excursions of justice" as he had come to call them, he was able to halt several crimes. Over the last week he stopped two private residences, a gas station, and the local chapter of the American Legion from being robbed. He also thwarted two carjackings and one attempt of lizard theft.

This last thief was caught almost by accident. Benji was on his way home and spotted a man trying to coax a large monitor lizard into the back of a waiting Chevy Trailblazer. When the driver of the SUV saw Benji approaching they sped off into the night, leaving their partner high and dry. He tried to flee on foot, but tripped over the big reptile and fell on his face. Without having to really use any of his special gadgets, Benji made sure both man and lizard were secure, and then notified the authorities. When the police arrived they found the lizard-napper in front of the zoo, plastic wrapped to a tree, and handcuffed to the large lizard with a pair of plastic garbage bag ties. When questioned, the thief gave the officers the name of his partner, and he was also apprehended.

Even though the event with the lizard was kind of comical, he was happy the crook was taken into custody. This was what he was most proud of. In all the crimes he had stopped, all criminals involved were now behind bars. Some instances, like with the monitor lizard, it was easy, while other times it took a serious confrontation to make sure the crooks would be arrested. This did not matter however, as all crimes great or small needed to be stopped if at all possible, and if they could not, then the least he could do was see that those involved were brought to justice.

With his exploits making the news, stories often finding themselves on the front page of the newspaper, he found himself starting to gain some notoriety. The publicity was all positive, and the citizens of Range City seemed to be rallying around his cause. With the reporter Brooks Quinlan fanning the flames on a daily basis, with upbeat articles cheering him on, his popularity was on the rise. This was exactly what he hoped would happen; through his actions and willingness to take a stand, the people of this city were rediscovering their hope.

He was also happy to discover he was the topic of conversation all around the city. Almost everywhere he went, he would overhear gossip and whisperings. There were, of course, the questions he'd expected about his identity, but those seemed to take a backseat to the overwhelming support he was garnering from the populace.

One of his new favorite pastimes was to visit The 18 Wheeler for coffee every morning, listening to the older customers as they discussed how he managed to catch the criminals. They would talk, argue, and laugh when discussing how he used cooking oil filled balloons to trip up one crook, or how another was found pinned to a tree with meat thermometers. Much to his delight, the old-timers got the biggest kick out of his pneumatic rifle, which they had dubbed the "plastic blaster."

It had only been a week, but everything seemed to be falling into place accordingly. His tools and devices were all working perfectly. The citizens were happy once again, and were supporting his cause. The newspaper was on his side and always asking for more. The crime rate was slowly starting to decline as word spread of his exploits. Up to this point, the police had left him alone and accepted the help he offered without question. His plan, so far, was a rousing success.

Tonight, he looked out over the city from his perch on the roof of the Midtown Coin Laundry. This was the first night since he began making his rounds he had sat idle for this length of time. This was a good sign, and he felt a sense of pride. It was far better to have a quiet evening though he had to admit to himself he was moderately disappointed. He really liked capturing criminals. It was still relatively early though, only nearing midnight, so there was still plenty of time for something to happen.

The lights switching off in the building across the street caught his attention. He had not noticed before, but the building was home to the *Range City Star Courier*. He wondered if maybe subconsciously he had been drawn to this site. With all the good press he was receiving it was only naturally his curiosity would be piqued.

He was still watcing the building when the front door opened and a young woman walked out. She had shoulder length brown hair that looked naturally curly, and dressed casually, wearing jeans and a sleeved blouse. She had a small purse slung over one shoulder and was carrying what looked like a laptop computer in her arms, similar to a student holding their textbooks. She stopped to adjust her glasses, then began digging through her purse until she pulled out a set of keys. Crossing the street, she approached a blue Toyota Camry parked in front of the laundromat. She must have unlocked it with a device on her keys because the lights blinked on and there was the unmistakable clicking sound. She continued walking to the car confidently unaware she was being watched.

A flash of motion in the shadows across the street near the newspaper building caught Benji's attention. Looking over, he could see a masked man sprinting across the pavement on an intercept course with the unsuspecting woman. Benji knew he had to move quick if he was going to have an opportunity to stop the masked man. Anyone wearing a dark ski mask at night, during summer, did not have good intentions on their mind.

From a side pouch in the backpack, he pulled out a re-worked pair of salad tongs he had reworked into a boomerang. The tongs were light weight metal, folded together, and with a flick of his wrist they sprang apart ready to be thrown. When angled just right, the boomerang would sweep around the attacker, taking him out.

With only seconds to spare, Benji stood up, aimed, and launched the salad tong boomerang. His aim was true, the one time serving tool smacked the would be attacker right in the knee. The crook was upended, going head over heels in a complete somersault, landing on his back. A loud "huh" sound escaped him as the air was forced from his lungs.

Wasting no time in case the perpetrator was able to regain his senses and try to flee or worse, Benji leapt off the roof, landing on an awning below. Using his momentum, he grabbed the front bar supporting the awning, and flipped over to land on his feet at the opposite side of the woman's Camry.

The masked man had found enough oxygen to try and get back to his feet, though Benji could tell he was still dazed. Not wanting to give the crook any more time to get his senses back, he grabbed his plastic blaster, and wrapped him in several tight layers of plastic wrap. Knowing the crook was incapacitated, he turned to the young woman who was now staring at him with eyes as big as saucers, "Are you alright ma'am?"

When she did not reply, he stepped around the rear of the car and stood directly in front of her, trying again. "Ma'am are you hurt?"

"What? Oh, yes, I'm fine," the woman answered, still staring at him in wide eyed amazement. "You're him aren't you? I can't believe it's really you."

Not sure how to respond, Benji stood his ground, offering up only a smile, which he knew was partially hidden by his helmet. "Well miss, if you are uninjured, I would suggest calling the police. I don't think your attacker is going anywhere soon, but better safe than sorry."

He continued watching her with a mixture of amusement at her reaction to his presence, and curiosity at her ability to remain calm even after nearly being assaulted. His curiosity grew as he saw her look in the direction of the wrapped up crook, and nonchalantly shrug her shoulders.

"He looks pretty tied up to me. I would rather talk to you if you have a few minutes."

"I'm flattered miss, but I need to be going. Crime waits for no one." He turned his back, and began to walk away, wishing he could make some sort of spectacular exit, but he was left with jogging down the street as his only option. He had just gotten back to the sidewalk, and was preparing to take off when the woman's voice stopped him.

"Please, just a few minutes of your time. My readers will be so excited if I can get some new information about you."

With renewed interest, he turned to stare at the woman reappraising her.

"Your readers?" he asked.

"Yes. Let me introduce myself, I'm Brooks Quinlan."

Now he was the one staring in amazement. "You're Brooks Quinlan… the reporter who's been writing the articles about me?"

"The one and same," she answered proudly. "Wait a minute, you read those?"

Feeling himself begin to redden from his embarrassment, he stammered, "I've, ah, seen them."

"That's fantastic! So will you let me ask you those questions?"

"I'd really like to help you Ms. Quinlan, but the less you know about me the better, I think."

A groan from the crook caught their attention.

"Now, I really think it's in your best interest to call the police."

"Please, just a few questions. I promise not to get too personal."

"Again, I must decline."

He was surprised, and more than a little caught off guard, when she ignored his refusal and instead walked around the car to stand in front of him in an attempt to cut off his retreat.

"Why the Army fatigues and kitchen utensils, when there have to be better ways to fight criminals?"

He shook his head at her tenacity. He had to admit that against his better judgment, he liked this reporter. His respect for her growing, he decided to give her a piece of vague information.

"If you must know, a man uses the tools he knows best."

He saw her eyes were growing wide once again, reflecting her surprise. He chuckled out loud before stepping around her. "Now, if you will excuse me, I must be going."

Before she was able to ask any more questions, he sprinted off down the street, darting into the first alley he came to. Locating his bike, he hopped on, fired it up, and sped away. Even though he had been out only a couple of hours, he decided to head back to the farm house. He knew the reporter, Quinlan, would likely try to find him, and he had no desire to answer any more of her questions. He did have a gut feeling that she would be a valuable person to have on his side. He may have to meet her again, but only on his terms.

The next morning, he stayed true to his routine as he awoke at eight in the morning, arriving at The 18 Wheeler by 9:15 a.m. He immediately noticed the idle chatter of the diner's customers was way above the normal roar; a buzz of excitement hung in the air. When the waitress brought him his first cup of coffee, his curiosity got the better of him.

"What is everyone in such an uproar about?"

The waitress poured the coffee before answering. "Haven't you seen the morning paper yet? That reporter, Quinlan, met the vigilante last night, and now we know his name."

A trickle of fear raced up his spine. Had he given away some unknown piece of information that had given his identity away? He looked at the newspaper rolled up on the table. He had bought it before entering the diner like always, and like always, he waited to open it up until he had gotten his coffee.

The waitress finished filling his cup, and moved on to the next customer. When she was away from his booth, he snatched the paper, smoothing it open with his forearm. When he saw the headline jumping out at him, the fear he was feeling dissipated, and was replaced by a sense of confused wonder.

It seemed Ms. Quinlan had taken it upon herself to christen him with a new name. The appropriateness of the moniker was perfect, and he smiled in spite of himself. It was going to be a whole new ballgame from now on. He took a careful sip of the hot coffee before diving into the rest of the article. He re-read the bold headline, nodding his head in approval. He had to admit it had a nice ring to it; he liked it.

There on the front page in the customary large block capital letters was the headline:

"RANGE CITY'S OWN HERO, CAPTAIN KITCHEN!"

CHAPTER 18

Discussion at City Hall

Police Chief Anderson walked the sidewalk to the City Hall building frustrated, knowing full well the mayor had summoned him to this impromptu meeting to discuss the vigilante the press had dubbed Captain Kitchen. In all of his fifty-five years, twenty-three of which were spent as a member of the Range City Police Department, he had never seen anything like this Captain Kitchen character. He did not know what the Mayor expected to hear, but he was pretty sure he did not have the answers.

The sun was shining brightly, and the whole city seemed different somehow. It was like the window he was used to seeing the city through had been washed and squeegee'd making the view sparkle with cleanliness. The veil of criminal activity was beginning to lift, and he knew this could be directly attributed to the work of Captain Kitchen. Whatever else the mayor was going to say about vigilantism being wrong, the chief was not going to let the man's melodrama get in the way of the important role and symbol Captain Kitchen portrayed.

The police already had their hands so full, criminals were slipping through the cracks. If this so called vigilante was able to help seal some of those cracks, then so much the better. With the no leads to the major bank robberies that were plaguing the city, he could use all the help he could get. Heck, this whole city could use the help.

He walked through the glass doors of City Hall with a chip starting to develop on his shoulder. He approached the metal detectors with a glare of fierce determination etched on his face. The two security guards standing there recognized the chief, and more importantly, recognized the serious look on his face. They waved him through the side, letting him skip the regular procedures.

The chief brushed past them with a brief nod of his head; he was a man on a mission, and he did not have time or the patience to play security games with the young guards. The nod was his way of showing them professional courtesy.

After passing the guard station, he hooked a quick right and found himself standing in front of a bank of elevators. The mayor's office was on the third floor. Normally, he would have taken the stairs as a way to get some exercise, but he wanted to be fresh and not out of breath when he met with Mayor Martinez. If he was going to have any shot of out-arguing the crafty politician he would need to be at his best, and walking into that meeting huffing and puffing like a beached whale, would not exactly project an aura of confidence.

He pushed the up button, and the elevator doors opened immediately with a welcoming ding. Stepping inside, he selected the third floor button, and the doors closed with another ding. Once sealed, the elevator whisked him upward at a pretty good clip; it had been some time since he had ridden the elevator, and he was caught off guard by the sudden motion. He grabbed the handrail to help compensate for the quick change in his balance. Soon, the elevator came to a jolting halt, and opened up. He exited, and stood still in the hallway for a few seconds to get his bearings back.

Mayor Martinez's office was located down the hall and around the corner. He had only been here a couple of times before, and those meetings were under better circumstances.

The office itself was set up similar to a doctor's. There was a decent-sized waiting room with several comfortable chairs, and a desk right as you walked in. The main difference was the color scheme. Where in a medical facility one would expect to see mild or soft colors with a lot of white, the mayor's office was colored a deep rich brown and mahogany. It gave credence to the idea of a sense of authority.

The mayor's secretary, Jennifer Samuelson, was seated behind the desk; a pretty thirty-something year old who was as dedicated as they came. She took her job as not just the mayor's secretary, but his personal assistant as well, incredibly serious. There were several inside jokes running around City Hall that Mrs. Samuelson was in fact the real power, and the mayor was simply a puppet. It was a tribute to the effectiveness with which she performed her duties. This morning, she was typing away on her computer keyboard at a rate which could have rivaled warp speed. He could almost convince himself he could see smoke rising from her fingers, and he actually thought he caught a feint whiff of burnt plastic.

"Good morning, Jen. I'm here to see the mayor, he's expecting me."

"Morning Chief, let me buzz him, and let him know you're here."

He smiled in response; he did not feel particularly friendly at the moment, but it would not help his cause any if he was to tick off the power behind the throne, so to speak.

"The mayor said to go on in."

"Thanks, Jen."

"Hey Chief, what you think about this Captain Kitchen business?"

He had already begun walking towards the heavy oak door. Without breaking stride, he looked over his shoulder and answered. "I'll let ya know officially after this meeting," he said with a hint of sarcasm.

Before he could reach out and grasp the door handle, it swung inward with an audible whoosh of air. The mayor was standing right inside the entrance, and welcomed him in with a sweep of his arm. "How are you doing this fine morning, Chief?"

Mayor Martinez was of average height and average build, dressed in his own uniform of duty - a navy blue suit, a white dress shirt, and a red tie. His jet-black hair was combed to one side, not one hair out of place. A perfectionist when it came to his personal appearance and his duties, his professional demeanor was always one thing the chief admired.

"I'm alright your honor, pretty busy though," he answered, hoping the mayor would get the not-so-subtle hint.

"Aren't we all these days," the mayor replied. "Let me get down to business. What do you know about this Captain Kitchen situation?"

"Well sir, to be honest, very little except in the last week he has been able to catch more criminals than my department has in the last month."

"Exactly!" the mayor exclaimed before walking around the large desk, and sitting down.

The chief could feel the blood rushing to his cheeks as his anger began to rise. They'd been doing all they could, but were outnumbered probably three to one out on the streets.

"Look here Mayor, my men are doing all they can."

"Yes Chief, your men should be commended for the work they have done. I think you misunderstood my tone. I was not trying to belittle the officers of this city's police force. I was only trying to emphasize the success our vigilante has been able to achieve."

With his interest now piqued, Chief Anderson took a chair facing the mayor. He was a little confused. He had been expecting a reprimand and some sort of an argument about how to handle the vigilante, Captain Kitchen. Now though, it seemed he and the mayor were on the same page. He continued to stare at the Mayor unsure how to respond.

"I can see by the look on your face Chief, you were expecting a different kind of meeting."

"Well to be honest sir, I wasn't really sure what to expect, but I had planned on arguing on the side of Captain Kitchen."

"I understand Chief, but desperate times call for desperate measures. This city is under siege, make no mistake about that. My office, City Hall, your police department... we've all worked diligently to stem the flow of criminal activity, but so far we have come up short. The only one who has shown results is this Captain Kitchen. The citizens love him, so I say more power to him."

Stunned by this unexpected turn of events, the chief paused before responding, "I couldn't agree with you more, sir."

"I'm glad we see eye to eye on this, Chief. I think our next step should be to reach out to him and try to open a dialogue, to begin a partnership. What do you think?"

"I'm right there with ya, sir."

"Good, any idea who he is?"

"None, but I haven't really looked very hard. I was thinking of contacting the reporter, Quinlan. She seems to know an awful lot about his activities."

"Good idea. Keep me up to date on any progress. I would love a chance to talk to this guy."

Feeling the meeting was coming to a close, Chief Anderson stood up, reached out his hand, and shook the Mayor's offered hand warmly before adding, "I will your Honor."

"Good day Chief, and keep up the good work."

He nodded happily before walking out of the office. As he trekked back down the hallway, down the elevator, and out the front door, he could not help but smile at his good fortune. The security guards must have thought he was Jekyll and Hyde as he walked by, but with the mayor on his side, and Captain Kitchen apprehending bad guys, things were really starting to look up.

As he got in his patrol car, and could see the bright sunshine streaming through the windshield he could not help but think what a glorious day it was.

CHAPTER 19

Where's the Mayor?

After his meeting with Chief Anderson, Mayor Martinez was feeling upbeat. The talk with the chief had gone better than expected, and the swiftness with which it was concluded left him with spare time in his schedule. Usually his later mornings were filled with a variety of appointments dealing with anything from budget concerns to ideas for new city ordinances.

He glanced over at the antique grandfather clock located in the far corner, and seeing it was nearing 11, decided to treat himself to an extended lunch break. He did not have anything else scheduled for a couple hours, and since free time was such a commodity, he was not going to feel guilty about indulging himself. He rarely, if ever, had time to take a good lunch break.

Still feeling excited about what appeared to be a bright, possibly crime-free future, he picked up the phone and paged Mrs. Samuelson. As usual, his secretary picked up after the first ring.

"Yes, sir?"

"Jennifer, I'm going out for a couple of hours. If I'm needed you can reach me on my private cell."

"No problem, sir. Enjoy your lunch."

He had to smile at his assistant's intuitiveness. He could never put one over on her. Though he liked to joke about it, he was actually a little worried she could really read his mind.

Two blocks away from City Hall, the Ice Cream Man set his plan into action; the listening device his minions had installed in the mayor's office allowed him to hear everything that transpired.

With the mayor going out for awhile, it was time to add kidnapping to his list of perfect crimes.

He pulled out a short range communication device, clicked a button on the side to opening up the receiver. There was a quiet burst of static before a voice answered.

"What are your orders, master?"

The evil Ice Cream Man smiled maliciously. He always loved being referred to as master. It was such an ego boost.

"It is time for phase two, the mayor is on the move. I will meet you at the rendezvous site."

"Yes, master," the voice on the other end of the communication device answered dreamily.

Everything was coming together nicely. As with his other plans, he was sure this one would work to perfection as well, so all he had to do now was sit back and wait. From his vantage point, he had a clear view of Civil Avenue, the street running in front of City Hall. When he finally saw what he had been waiting for, he started the ice cream truck, and pulled into traffic.

When the elevator doors opened up, Mayor Martinez stepped out into the stale air of the parking garage. Mrs. Samuelson had no doubt called ahead so his car would be ready and waiting for him. As if on cue, a navy blue Seville came into view, halting in front of the elevators. A young man crawled out of the driver's seat and opened the rear driver's side door for the mayor to get in. This was a familiar scenario for Mayor Martinez, but something seemed out of sorts.

"Thank you, young man, but where is my usual driver?"

"He had a family emergency sir. He had to leave rather suddenly and I was asked to fill in."

"Oh, I see. Well, I hope everything is all right."

"As do I, sir."

"I didn't catch your name."

"It's Todd Stevens."

"That name sounds familiar. Have we met before?"

"I don't believe so, sir."

There was something odd about the young driver's demeanor. He was friendly enough, but all his answers were flat and unemotional. If he didn't know better, the mayor would have thought the man to be in a trance of some sort, an utterly ridiculous notion. It was more likely the driver was nervous, he was about to become the personal driver for the mayor, after all.

Deciding not to push the issue further, Mayor Martinez climbed into the back seat of the car, ready for his extended lunch. He still watched the driver curiously though; there was something oddly familiar about the young lad, but he could not quite put his finger on it. He was awfully young to be an employee for City Hall, but that was not what was causing his trepidation. As the car pulled out of the garage into the sunny late morning, the Mayor's mind began to wander. Instead of focusing on the driver's strange behavior, his thoughts began to drift to what he would have to eat for lunch. A large pepperoni pizza with extra cheese would hit the spot.

The car came to a stop at a traffic light, and that's when it hit him. Now he knew why the driver looked so familiar—it was the same kid who had gotten arrested for doing cannonballs in his underwear into his fountain.

"Hey, I remember you now."

The driver turned around, still with the blank expression on his face. He held up his hand, holding what looked like a small breath freshener spray, and squirted it into the mayor's face.

"What the…" the mayor began, confused. "What was that? What do you think you're…?" Before he could finish his thought, he slumped over on the backseat snoring loudly.

When the light turned green, the driver accelerated, paying no attention to the passenger lying unconscious in the back seat. The only thing Todd Stevens focused on were the orders he had been given to meet at the rendezvous spot. Those orders were the only thing that mattered.

He did not pay attention to anything else, not even the ice cream truck following closely behind.

When the mayor's secretary and personal assistant returned from her own lunch sometime later, she found it strange the mayor himself had yet to return. This was unlike him, and he did have a meeting scheduled; the mayor never missed a meeting.

Her curiosity up, she called down to the garage to check and see if Mayor Martinez had returned. When nobody answered, she got worried. Someone was supposed to be on duty at all times down there. She should have known something was up earlier, when she hadn't recognized the voice of the person answering when she had called earlier to have the car ready.

She decided to dial the mayor's private cell phone so she could ease her mind, waiting while the phone rang three times. When she heard the sinister voice on the other end answer, she was nowhere near being at ease.

"Hello Mrs. Samuelson. How nice of you to check in on your boss," the Ice Cream Man said mockingly. "Listen carefully because I am going to say this only once. At 7 p.m. tonight, I will broadcast to the citizens of Range City my demands concerning their beloved mayor. Any attempts to locate me before that time will not bode well for the continued good health of the honorable Mayor Martinez. If they do try, I will know. Until 7 p.m. then, Mrs. Samuelson, I bid you a good day."

She stood in complete shock, holding the phone in a death grip. After the initial surprise wore off, she dialed the extension to Chief Anderson. After a couple of rings he picked up. "Hello, Chief. This is Jennifer Samuelson. We have a situation."

CHAPTER 20

A Televised Ransom

After putting the finishing touches on a new whisk bolas, Benji decided to get cleaned up and grab a quick bite to eat before heading out for his evening patrol. He walked the short distance from the machine shop to the farmhouse happily whistling the chorus from an All American Reject song he had heard earlier in the day.

The house was quiet as usual; the stillness of the place always bothered him so on his way in to the kitchen, he stopped and turned on the television. Though he rarely watched TV anymore, he found the background noise it provided to be comforting.

He glanced at the clock sitting on the mantle of the fireplace, and noticing it was close to 7 p.m., he grabbed the remote from the coffee table and switched to Channel 8 so he could catch the weather forecast and last smidgen of news. This way maybe he could get an early heads up on where to concentrate his efforts for the evening's work.

He noted the news was on a commercial break as he hit the volume button on the remote, turning the sound up loud enough for him to hear in the other room. Then he went to the kitchen to make a much needed snack.

He had just finished constructing his sandwich when the sound of the anchor's voice caught his attention. Not so much the sound, as it was the tone. Though he could not quite make out the newsman's muffled words, he could tell by the seriousness with which the anchorman was speaking that something dire had happened.

Sandwich in hand, he returned to the living room to better hear the news, but paused in mid-bite as he heard the story.

"To recap the situation for those just joining us," the anchorman began ominously. "The Range City Police Department and officials at City Hall have both confirmed that sometime between 11 a.m. and 1 p.m. today, Mayor Joseph Martinez was kidnapped by as of yet unidentified kidnapper or kidnappers, who will broadcast a message at 7 p.m. Mrs. Jennifer Samuelson, the long-time aide of Mayor Martinez, was given these instructions when she tried to contact the Mayor on his private cell phone, and was instead connected with the mayor's abductor. No further information has been given at this time. The Range City Police Chief Derrick Anderson, along with city officials, will be holding a press conference after the kidnapper's demands are known. We should be getting word concerning the impending broadcast within the next ten minutes. Again, to re-iterate, Mayor Joseph Martinez has been the target of an apparent kidnapping."

The sandwich fell from Benji's hand as the weight of the news began to sink in. He stood transfixed, staring at the television as the anchor began re-telling the story. This was completely unheard of. What possible reason would anyone in their right mind have to kidnap the mayor? The whole idea seemed ludicrous.

He glanced at the clock once more, and seeing it was mere minutes before the kidnapper's broadcast, knew he would not have long to wait for his answer.

Across town, the mayor woke to find himself in a laboratory that could have graced the cover of Mad Scientist Weekly, if such a magazine existed. He was still a bit groggy, and surprised to find he was secured tightly to a chair; his arms were strapped to the armrests of the chair with heavy leather, his legs were tied together at the ankles, with what he could only assume to be a similar leather strap. In his current state he was completely immobilized.

The sound of footsteps approaching from directly behind him caught his attention.

"Who's there? What is the meaning of all this?" he questioned.

"Ah, Mayor, I see you have awakened from your little nap," a voice answered, sounding like the hiss of a snake. "I take it you rested comfortably."

"Show yourself. I demand to know who you are and why I have been taken," the mayor said, voice rising in fear and anger.

"For a man in your rather secured predicament Mayor, I would watch your tone. From where I am standing you are in no position to demand anything." The Ice Cream Man crossed in front of the chair, and stared down at his prisoner. "As for whom I am, names are not important, but if you must, you may call me the Ice Cream Man. And as for why you are here, my dear Mayor, well you are going to help me with a little project."

The mayor could only stare back at his captor. The mysterious figure was dressed completely in black, including black boots, gloves, and a wide-brimmed hat similar to what he had seen pictures of Amish men wearing. The man was also wearing a long black trench coat, with an equally black mask covering his mouth, perhaps partially the cause for the hissing quality to his voice. He also wore a pair of mirrored sunglasses, so when he looked at his face, all the Mayor could see was his own helpless reflection. He guessed the outfit was more for show than anything else, a means to intimidate him far more than he already was.

The mayor was left speechless at the sight of the eerie Ice Cream Man. The bravado he felt moments before melted away like the namesake of his captor would on a hot summer's day. All he could do was stare, open-mouthed, at the strange figure before him. He was completely helpless and his captor knew it.

"I see the proverbial cat has gotten your tongue, my dear mayor. You should be glad. There are far worse things that can be done to a tongue that wags too often."

Getting the meaning of the veiled threat, Mayor Martinez gulped audibly out of fear.

"Enough witty banter mayor, it is almost time for our big coming out party. You will love this, you are one of the guests of honor."

The evil Ice Cream Man grabbed the arms of the chair, pausing briefly to stare at his helpless captive, and spun the chair around before pushing it out of the lab.

The mayor was taken aback when he was wheeled into what appeared to be a makeshift TV studio. There were lamps angled around the room to help with lighting, and an expensive looking camera set on a tripod facing he and his captor.

"Now, be a good little public official, and smile pretty for the camera. This is our big moment. You wouldn't want to disappoint your adoring public would you?"

"You're crazy," the mayor said, his horror deepening.

The Ice Cream Man glared coldly at his prisoner, before taking a different approach. "Tut... tut Mayor, didn't your mother ever teach you about having manners? It is quite rude to call your host such unsavory names," the Ice Cream Man said menacingly.

Pausing a moment, the Ice Cream man chuckled at before asking, "Perhaps you are thirsty, may I bring you something cool to drink?" Without waiting for an answer, the Ice Cream Man disappeared, leaving the mayor alone in the studio. The man was obviously unbalanced, but how much so was a question he was not sure he wanted answered.

When the Ice Cream Man returned, the major could see his captor was holding a glass of greenish liquid in his black gloved hand. "Here Mayor, drink up. This will help you to relax," the Ice Cream Man said jokingly, though there was no way to hide the evil intent in his voice.

Before he could even respond, the black clad villain pounced on the mayor, forced open his mouth, and poured the vile green fluid down his throat. The taste was overwhelmingly bitter, and had the villainous Ice Cream Man not been holding his mouth closed, he would have thrown the disgusting liquid up in his captor's black masked face.

After the initial shock of the horrible taste wore off, he began to feel drowsy, and a warm sensation came over his body, he felt almost as if he were floating on air. It was not an unpleasant feeling, but there was a warning siren going off deep in his subconscious mind. Before he could heed the warning and try to fight the insidious effects of the liquid, it was too late. The mind control formula had taken effect, claiming its newest victim.

Benji was lost in thought, determining how best to react to this disturbing development, when the voice of the anchor brought him back to the here and now.

"This just in. The Channel 8 studio has received a live feed from the supposed kidnapper. We will be transferring to this feed shortly."

He did not even blink as he watched the screen switch from the familiar Channel 8 news room to a poorly lit, amateurish studio. There were only two figures on screen; one was Mayor Martinez looking as if he had been drugged, and the other was a mysterious figure, dressed all in black, who gave off an aura of evil.

Benji found having a seat on his couch, completely entranced by the scene unfolding on the television. He actually sucked in a sharp breath as the strange figure began to speak.

"Citizens of Range City, I am the Ice Cream Man. As you can see, the Honorable Mayor Martinez is currently my... guest. Do not worry, he has not been harmed... yet. Over the last several weeks I have masterminded many crimes against the financial institutions of your fair city. With the help of my minions, I now control the financial fortunes of every person living in Range City. I have also, as you can see, taken the Mayor against his will. I have been able to pull off these unbelievable crimes with a perfect precision that has left the law enforcement agencies of Range City looking foolish. I can strike anywhere and at anytime. My ability to commit these criminal acts knows no bounds.

"My demand is a simple one. Once ownership and decision making power of Range City is transferred to me, I will release the Mayor and return enough funds so the citizens may return to their otherwise meaningless lives and routines. As an added incentive I have taken the liberty of arranging the captivity of fifty more hostages. I am certain the identity of these young hostages will be realized shortly. I give the city council twenty-four hours to make a decision. After that, the Mayor and other hostages will disappear, forever. Any attempt to locate me or apprehend me in any way will be seen as a refusal of my demand, and will result in dire consequences. All communication coming into and leaving the city is being monitored. I have eyes and ears everywhere. Your twenty-four hours begins now."

After the last statement, the feed was cut unceremoniously. There were a few seconds of blank screen and dead air before the Channel 8 newsroom once again filled the screen. The anchor was talking, but Benji did not hear a word.

If ever there was a time the city needed a hero, it was now. He did not think he would be able to do it alone, however. If there was going to be any hope of saving the hostages, and the city itself, he would have to reach out to the Range City Police Department. Together, they just may be able to put a stop to this villain's evil plan.

He would have to start at the top, and pay a visit to Chief Anderson. He had actually planned on reaching out to the chief in the near future, once he was completely accepted by the citizens of R.ange City, and it would seem fate had intervened in his life once again, however, as the important meeting with Chief Anderson would have to take place tonight.

With no more time to waste, he ran out to the machine shop to get dressed; he had not a moment to spare as the clock to the twenty-four hour deadline had begun ticking. It was time to go to work. He had a city to save.

Chapter 21

A Friendship Forged

Benji decided to forego his usual stealth, and parked his motorcycle right in front of the police station. He knew his appearance would more than likely cause a stir the moment he walked through the doors, and he wasn't disappointed.

At first none of the officers working the front desk seemed to notice. Then, almost as one, they stopped what they were doing, and stood completely still. Where seconds before the entrance was filled with the noisy commotion of officers working in a crisis, it was now so quiet you could have heard a pin drop. "I need to see the Chief," he said, as confidently as he could, hoping this simple statement would be enough to break the spell.

His request alone was not enough to bring the officers back to the here and now. It took the incessant ringing of more than one phone to pull them back to a respectable level of consciousness. He could hear brief snippets of conversation as the phone calls were answered.

"Yes ma'am, I assure you we are doing everything we can."

"I promise we will not let any harm come to your son."

"We have the entire department working on this."

Benji assumed these calls were in reference to the fifty other hostages the villainous Ice Cream Man mentioned, and from what he was able to hear, it sounded as if the calls were coming from concerned parents. If the other hostages were children, that added a whole new dimension of trouble to the already impossible dilemma.

With the initial shock his appearance caused over, he was surprised to find he was now being ignored. He was about to reiterate his request when one officer in particular caught his attentionand he watched as a young desk sergeant slammed down a phone in frustration and called out down the hall behind him, "Hey Chief, we got another one."

Chief Anderson walked out of his office and headed to the front desk. Benji waited until the chief was within earshot before calling out to him. "Chief Anderson, I believe we need to speak."

When the chief had entered the room, it looked as if someone let the air out of his body, veteran officer's shoulders were slumped and his body sort of sagged. The man look exhausted and on the edge of a nervous breakdown. After getting the report from the desk sergeant his appearance looked even more haggard, but when he heard his name called, the chief turned to see Benji, in all of his costumed glory, and actually seemed to perk up slightly.

"Under the circumstances, I should probably be torqued off to see you. I am out of ideas for this, so come on," the chief said, waving him back.

Benji waited as one of the desk officers let him through, the followed the chief into his office. It was smaller than Benji would have thought, and sparsely furnished; a desk littered with papers and files, a small loveseat against one wall, and two chairs set in front of the desk.

The two men stared at each other over that desk not sure how to break the ice. Neither man had use for small talk and pleasantries, as they both hosted action-orientated personalities, leaving them somewhat at a loss in a situation such as this. Benji opened his mouth to speak, still having no idea what to say. Closing his mouth again, he blew out a shallow breath.

"I don't know who you are, but I can tell you straight up I don't have time for games," Chief Anderson said, getting the conversational ball rolling.

"I don't much care for games myself, Chief," Benji replied, his tone heavy with concern over the seriousness of the situation. "I am here to help."

"Well, I can use all of that I can get right about now." The chief sighed.

"Tell me what you already know, and we can go from there."

"Follow me, and we'll talk as we walk," the chief replied.

Benji did as he was told, following the chief out of the office and down a hall while listening intently as he laid out what information the police already had.

"We don't really know anything about this Ice Cream Man guy. He claims to be the person responsible for all of the recent bank robberies, and we have no reason not to believe him. We do believe he has at least one accomplice, and that person, posing as a driver, is the one who did the actual kidnapping. For all we know, this whacko could have a whole army stashed away someplace." The chief paused in his summary as they entered a large conference room, filled with several other officers, a large board covered in pictures, and papers strewn about. Several of the officers were manning telephones while others were working through papers and guzzling coffee as fast as they could fill their cups.

When Benji walked in, he caused the same reaction as he had at the front desk. Everything seemed to stop at once. One officer even stopped in mid-sip with his cup of coffee in front of his mouth.

"Easy guys," the chief admonished. "He's a friend of mine."

This seemed to put everyone somewhat at ease, the officers picking up where they left off. Benji was somewhat amazed at how easily the other officers accepted the chief's explanation. There were no questions, just loyal men hard at work.

"Is there anything else you have to go on?" he asked the chief curiously.

"Only that he has made good on his threat of taking more hostages," the chief answered, moving to stand in front of the board containing the photos. "We have been receiving calls from parents ever since the demands aired. It seems kids ranging in ages thirteen to seventeen have been disappearing, and according to Sergeant Miller at the front desk, we got a new one."

This last bit of information caused the officers throughout the room to groan out of frustration in unison.

The chief finished his statement by gesturing toward the board. Benji's gaze followed, looking closely at all the pictures. One particular photo of a young boy caused a sense of familiarity. He stared a few seconds, trying to recall where he had seen the boy before, when all of a sudden it dawned on him. This was the same youth he had seen slip down the manhole on his first night as Captain Kitchen.

"I know this young man. I've seen him before," he said, getting an eerie feeling about these new hostages.

"If you have any information, we need to hear it," the chief replied.

"I think I might know how to find this guy, Chief." Benji watched as a range of emotions played out on Chief Anderson's lined face. If the situation had not been so serious, he would have chuckled out loud.

"How?" the chief asked in amazement.

"First answer a question for me. What is under this city?"

"This used to be an old mining town. It's riddled with old tunnels, but they have been shut down for years. When the sewer system was put in, most of those old tunnels were locked up," the chief answered, an edge of curiosity creeping into his voice.

"Those tunnels are how he is getting around undetected, and I don't think these fifty kids are hostages so much as they are somehow unwilling accomplices."

"I can't believe that. There are hundreds of tunnels down there. There is no way to track through them all without getting lost."

"I know this is hard for you, Chief, but I am asking you to trust me on this."

The moment of truth; either the Chief would trust him and a friendly partnership could be forged, or the veteran cop would dismiss him outright, causing a rift that would probably never be mended. He watched as the chief quietly and quickly thought things through. Benji knew this would not be an easy decision for the chief to make, especially here in front of his men.

After several minutes of concentration, the chief took several deep breaths, and replied. "Alright, at this point what do I have to lose. I still don't see how we can maneuver through those tunnels."

Benji nearly jumped with joy when he realized the chief was going to work with him. He had the distinct feeling that in the years to come he would be able to look back on this moment as the stepping stone leading to the path of justice. "Do you have access to dogs that can trail a scent?"

A large smile played out on the chief's face before the grizzled veteran called out to one of the officers working the phones.

"Get Dean Richards on the line. We have need of a couple of his bloodhounds."

CHAPTER 22

The Hunt Is On

Within one hour of his impromptu meeting with Chief Anderson, Benji once again found himself on Cook Street. Though it had been a few short weeks since he had spent his first night here, fighting three robbers, it felt like a lifetime had passed. So much had transpired since that time, it was hard to imagine what his life had even been like before taking up the mantle of Captain Kitchen. In an odd way, all his previous expectations had culminated to this moment.

He, Chief Anderson, and three officers were standing around the manhole cover he had seen the boy identified as Steven Arrington slip through on that first night. They were awaiting the arrival of Dean Richards and his hounds. At last count, fifty families had called in to the police station, marking all fifty of the Ice Cream Man's hostages. As soon as Richards and his dogs arrived, they would enter the labyrinth of tunnels below the city, in hopes of tracking the kidnapping villain to his secret lair.

The quicker they could find this lunatic, the better. His demand of being given power over the city was absolutely ridiculous, but with the mayor and fifty of the city's teenagers as hostages, they were not in a position to bargain. Benji knew the twenty-four hour deadline was merely a formality. The Ice Cream Man was obviously not playing with a full deck, and could do something irrational at any moment. They simply could not take any chances with so many lives at stake. If this plan worked, they just might have a chance.

The sound of an approaching vehicle drew him back to the current situation. He watched as an unremarkable green van came into view, slowing as it neared, pulling over to the curb to park. The van rattled and shook for a few seconds before the engine came to a complete stop.

"It's about time," Benji heard the chief utter.

He took this to mean Dean Richards had finally arrived. Even though the man had been contacted while they were still at the station, it had taken over an hour for him to arrive. He was surprised by how young the man was, no more than his late twenties, but according to the chief, he bred the best bloodhounds in the entire county, possibly even the state. The chief also warned that Richards was a little on the strange side, but was very professional when it came to his dogs.

Richards himself looked like the poster child for what was referred to as "emo punk." He was dressed in black combat boots similar to what Benji himself was wearing, and black pants with a series of buckles all over them. He was also wearing a sleeveless white muscle shirt with the phrase "Parental Advisory" in big black letters. His wrists were covered in a variety of bracelets that looked like miniature versions of the spiked dog collars his hounds were wearing. He had his nose, eyebrow, and lip pierced, with hoops hanging from each. His hair, obviously dyed jet black, was long in front so it hung in his eyes, but shaved on the sides and back. He shuffled as he walked, shoulders slumped as if they were carrying the weight of the world.

"Hey Chief, sorry I'm late. I was redoing my MySpace page and lost track of time," he said in a quiet voice.

"Well I hate to tear you away from the internet Dean, but we have some hostages we need to find," the chief responded in exasperation.

The dog owner did not even seem to pick up on the chief's sarcasm. Instead he took a look at Benji, asking, "Who's the guy in the goofy suit?"

"Funny, I was just about to ask the same thing," Benji replied jokingly.

The young man only shrugged his shoulders in response, barely acknowledging that a serious event was taking place. "I guess I'll go get my dogs ready."

"Good idea, Dean, you do that," the chief said, his patience running out.

When Dean had walked far enough away to be out of hearing range, Benji asked, "Are you sure this guy is with it enough to help?"

"I know Richards is odd as a cod, but his dogs really are the best," the chief answered.

There were two dogs, and Benji could see they were excited but ready to work, pulling hard on their leads as they made their way to the manhole.

"You got something they can get a scent from, Chief?" Richards asked.

"Yeah, I had Steven's mother drop this off as the station," the chief replied, producing a plain white t-shirt from his coat pocket. "According to her, Steven wore this to bed last night."

"Are you sure they can find his trail?" Benji asked. "I mean it is well over a week old."

"Trust me, if that kid went down this hole, my dogs will find him," Richards answered proudly.

Benji watched as Richards took the shirt from the chief and held it in front of the dogs' noses. They seemed to look at the garment curiously as they sniffed it, before turning their noses to the ground and taking up a loud baying, signalling they had the scent. The two bloodhounds headed straight for the manhole and began pawing at it with their feet.

"See, I told ya," Richards commented.

Benji waited anxiously as the chief contacted the station to let them know they were about to enter the tunnels, and to be ready with back-up when called. Two other officers quickly removed the manhole cover, which led to a new round of excited barking from the dogs. They had the scent for sure now, and were ready to go.

Peering down into the hole was useless as it was pitch black. The smell reminded Benji of his old storm cellar at home; the aroma of old bricks, dirt, and stale air was overwhelming at first, but it did not seem to bother the dogs. If it had not been for their owner holding on to them so tightly, he was sure they would have jumped head first into the hole. As it was, they had to be carried down by the chief's men, with Dean Richards following close behind like a worried mother concerned about the safety of her babies.

Once they were all down the hole, the chief gave Richards the okay to let the dogs move out. They were technically not in the old tunnels yet, and they would have to maneuver through the sewer system until they found a junction that would allow them to enter the old mine. Hopefully the two bloodhounds would lead them right to this junction.

Richards' dogs, true to form, took off like two red bullets, though they were surprisingly quiet as they led the way down the tunnel. If not for the flashlights the chief and his men were using, it would have been black as night, and with what little illumination the flashlights provided, Benji could barely see more than a few feet in front of him. The dogs seemed to know where they were going however, and the pace was fairly quick.

After roughly fifteen minutes, they came to the junction which would give them access to the long forgotten mine shafts. Once again there was a manhole cover marking the entrance, and when the officers shone their lights onto the cover, Benji could see the drag marks plainly from where the cover had recently been used. This was enough evidence for the chief, and he ordered this lid opened as well.

This time it only took one officer to pull the manhole cover off. There was a burst of hot air bringing with it the stench of a long lost crypt. All six men looked at each other, unsure how to proceed.

"After you, Chief," Benji said jokingly, trying to relieve some of the tension of the moment.

"I don't think so," the chief replied. "You're supposed to be the hero remember."

Benji chuckled and shook his head. "You would have to remind me of that."

"Hey, you're the one with the funny costume," the chief said, playing along.

Not wanting to waste anymore precious time, Benji held out his hand, motioning for a flashlight. One was handed over, and he shone the beam of light down the hole, and still could not see how far down it went. There was an old wooden ladder leading down into the blackness, and with a last look at the chief, who gave him a wink of confidence, he climbed down.

The ladder was old, but sturdy. It creaked and groaned in protest, but held his weight with no problem. After climbing down approximately fifteen feet, he touched ground. He flashed the light to both his right and left, but it barely pierced the darkness. The tunnels were nothing more than rock and dirt, and the whole thing had a medieval dungeon feel to it. He had a hard time envisioning two young teenagers traversing these tunnels alone, at least not of their own free will. This evil Ice Cream Man must have some hold over these teenagers, and the other forty-eight he was supposedly holding as hostages.

"It's all clear down here, but watch the ladder. It's old but feels strong," he called up to the others.

Within a few minutes everyone had managed to climb down. The bloodhounds were once again carried down by Chief Anderson's men, and once they were huddled together, Dean Richards let the dogs smell the shirt belonging to Steven Arrington again. The two quickly took up the scent, and they moved off into the darkness.

The mine shafts were a virtual maze of tunnels crisscrossing the entire length of Range City. The minutes ticked by as the bloodhounds wound their way through the labyrinth. Benji and the rest of the search party had no idea where they were at, or how many miles they may have traveled. The tunnels seemed to go on forever, but the dogs never faltered.

After what could have been hours, or days for all he could tell after being in the dark for so long, the dogs led them into a new tunnel. The difference to this one was a light seen in the distance. He and the chief shared a look, knowing their journey was quite possibly coming to an end.

As they neared the light, he noticed this part of the tunnel had been reworked with extra supports, along with a modern lighting system. The tunnel itself branched off to the right, and he could tell that part was well-lit as well.

The chief tapped him on the shoulder, and when he turned he could see the chief waving the others close. Once everyone was leaning in, he started doling out instructions. "Everyone listen. There is no way these lights should be here. According to the dogs, we are headed in the right direction, and if Captain Kitchen's hunch is correct, we should be close to the Ice Cream Man's hideout. Dean, I want you and Officer Daniels to head back to the surface. I checked my cell phone, and I have no signal. Once you get back up top, I want you to get some back-up. If I can, I will try to contact the department. If I can't, then you two will be the only ones who will know how to find us. The rest of us will go on, and if the opportunity should present itself, save the mayor. Does everyone understand?"

Everyone nodded their assent when the chief stopped talking. Dean Richards and Officer Daniels, one of the three policemen in the group, turned and disappeared swiftly, back into the darkness from which they had come.

When they were completely out of sight, the chief motioned for the others to move out as well. They walked the rest of the way down the tunnel, and turned the corner only to find themselves in another long, well-lit shaft. This one, however, ended in a dead-end.

When Benji, the chief, and the two officers reached the end of the tunnel, he noticed an electric pad with one red button set into the stone of the tunnel wall. Seeing no other choice, he pushed the button. There was a rumbling sound, and all four men jumped back in surprise as the dead-end opened up to reveal the elevator hidden within.

"Shall we?" he asked.

"Why not," the chief replied. "We've come this far."

When all four men boarded the elevator, Benji reached out and pushed the button marked with the letter "L." The doors slid shut without a sound, and the elevator jerked into motion, taking them up. He had no idea how far the elevator traveled before it came to a halt.

He tensed in preparation, grabbing the handles of his frying pan clubs, not knowing what to expect as the doors opened. When they finally did slide open, he along with the Range City police officers, stepped out into a laboratory. The sound of cackling laughter caught them all by surprise.

"What took you so long?" the Ice Cream Man asked. "My minions and I have been waiting for you."

CHAPTER 23

Confrontation

The sound of the Ice Cream Man's voice and the sudden appearance of his black clad form took Benji and the police officers completely by surprise. They froze in place, not sure on how to proceed. Even more disturbing, he was not alone; at least ten of the missing teenagers stood around him.

"Chief Anderson, I am so glad you and your men could stop by, and I see you brought a guest along as well," the Ice Cream Man spoke, his voice filled with false pleasantries. Turning his attention to Benji he continued. "You must be the illustrious Captain Kitchen I have been reading so much about. I was planning on paying you a visit soon, but this will work so much the better."

The initial shock of being unexpectedly confronted by their adversary was starting to wear off the chief and his men. Benji could tell their training was beginning to take over as the three officers fanned out in an attempt to cover the Ice Cream Man from all angles.

"Alright Ice Cream Man, or whoever you are, this game of yours is over," the chief began. "Release the kids and the mayor and surrender peacefully."

"Oh, my dear Chief, you actually think you have a chance of stopping me, don't you? How quaint. You poor misguided old fool, you think I haven't planned for this contingency? You and your men have reacted precisely as I have anticipated. It is you who will surrender, or pay the direst of consequences," the Ice Cream Man responded, a hint of anger creeping into his otherwise calm voice.

Benji could see things were rapidly deteriorating, the tension level in the strange laboratory was increasing steadily with each passing second. There was too much at stake to let things get out of hand; the crazed villain was already using ten of the fifty hostages as human shields. They too, had that dreamy, faraway look in their eyes like he had seen in the mayor's eyes when the Ice Cream Man first made his demands. This told him that they were under some kind of spell, merely puppets at this point, and the Ice Cream Man was the one pulling the strings.

He was about to intervene in an attempt to keep the situation as calm and under control as possible, when one of the chief's officers—thinking he was in a good enough position—unholstered his firearm, and pointed it at the villain. "Hands up and on your knees, *now*."

The Ice Cream Man, still somewhat hidden behind the teenagers, made a flick of the wrist motion, shooting forth two electrical darts much like a taser gun. The darts hit the officer with the gun square in the chest, sending immobilizing volts of electricity into him. The officer grunted in pain before falling over on his side, muscles spasming from the electrical overload.

The chief and the other officer, seeing their comrade attacked, also drew their weapons and began to charge. They were too late however, as the Ice Cream Man tossed a glass vial shattering onto the ground, setting off a chemical reaction that caused the laboratory to quickly fill with a thick, pungent smoke. With almost no visibility, the chief and his officer were forced to stand their ground.

The Ice Cream Man used the cover of the smoke to disappear. The ten teenage hostages turned on the policemen by grabbing whatever was within reach, and throwing the items with all their might. The chief was quickly overcome by the bombardment of glass beakers and other laboratory equipment.

Benji knew he had to stop the kids before the chief and the other officer were injured, but he did not to harm them, so he did the only thing he could think of. He grabbed his plastic blaster, thumbed it on, and fired at the kids. Within seconds the laboratory floor was covered with what looked like overgrown plastic caterpillars.

The chief and the other officer took advantage of the reprieve Benji gave them, and made their way to the downed officer. He quickly followed suit, stumbling through the smoky lab and arriving at the injured man at the same time. He did not seem to be seriously hurt, but he was unconscious.

"You might try and call for that back-up now, Chief," Benji said.

"Good idea," the chief responded reaching for his cell phone.

"I'm going after the Ice Cream Man. I'll do my best to keep him busy long enough so you can get to the mayor and the other hostages. Be careful though, Chief, he has some sort of hold over those kids."

"You don't have to tell me," the chief said, rubbing his head where he had been hit by a flying beaker.

"Take it easy on the kids, Chief, I think he has drugged them somehow," Benji advised, and with a last look at the unconscious officer, he took off to stop the Ice Cream Man, once and for all.

CHAPTER 24

The Final Showdown

Once he fled the lab, the dreaded Ice Cream Man made his way to a storage unit where he kept the processed mind control formula. He grabbed two small vials that were still in their pure form. With these he planned on making Captain Kitchen his permanent servant.

He opened his coat to reveal a bandolier criss-crossed across his chest. Instead of bullets however, the bandolier contained several vials, each filled with one of the many different concoctions he had invented. He slipped the two vials of formula into empty slots. Now that he was fully armed, he was ready to make his stand.

He knew his best bet would be to face down Captain Kitchen with a prisoner in tow. He would need to get Mayor Martinez. With the mayor by his side, that wannabe superhero would think twice before doing anything rash. He smiled evilly, charging out into the corridor.

Benji exited the lab right as his adversary stepped back into the hall. He reached for his plastic blaster in hopes of being able to end this quickly.

"Alright Ice Cream Man, this craziness ends now."

He watched as the villain stopped in his tracks, slowly turning so they were facing each other. They both stood motionless, staring at each other, a futuristic version of an old west showdown.

"I don't think so, fool. The craziness is just getting started," the Ice Cream Man said, flicking his wrist, sending out more electric darts, this time in Benji's direction.

He was ready for this trick, and threw himself to the floor, allowing the darts to fly past him harmlessly. He fired the plastic blaster as he fell, but his aim was off, and the plastic wrap bounced off the wall next to the evil villain. The Ice Cream Man, to his credit, reacted swiftly by dropping to one knee, and pulled out two glass test tubes.

Benji was scrambling back to his feet when the Ice Cream Man threw the first vial. The glass container hit the wall next to Benji and shattered, spraying him with a sickly, sweet-smelling liquid. He was about to chase his opponent down when he began to swoon, and had to reach out to grab the wall to keep from falling over. Whatever the liquid was, it was causing his head to spin; he knew he would have to keep moving or he would more than likely pass out.

He grabbed his apron/cape and used it to wipe off what remained of the liquid as he slipped out his pot lid throwing discs. Gathering his strength, he threw the discs after the Ice Cream Man, who was trying to flee down the hall.

All three discs hit home. One caught the fleeing villain high on the shoulder, while the other two clipped him in the back of his legs, dropping him to his knees. Benji did not hesitate, and charged after his fallen foe.

When he was within a couple of feet, he prepared to fire the plastic blaster, but the Ice Cream Man turned and heaved a second vial. It hit the plastic blaster, breaking and covering the weapon in sticky goo that hardened immediately, making the blaster useless. Benji could hear the evil Ice Cream Man laughing with glee at his predicament.

"Oh, how the mighty have fallen," the Ice Cream Man said tauntingly. "Did you really think your simple little tools could best my superior intellect?"

"They may be simple, but you will find they are quite effective," Benji replied as he fired the pepper spoon from his bracer.

The Ice Cream man was so busy gloating, he was caught completely unaware and grunted in surprise as well as pain when the spoon hit him directly in the forehead. The villain sneezed once from the pepper, and fell backwards, landing on his butt.

Seeing his chance, Benji pulled out his frying pan nightsticks, and moved in to finish off the villain before any more damage could be done. Even so, he was not quick enough; the vile criminal mastermind produced yet another vial, flinging the contents directly into his face as he approached.

Benji's eyes began to sting and burn, then he began coughing and gagging as the contents worked their way down his throat. The next thing he knew, he could not hear, and the aroma of the subterranean passageway disappeared. He dropped the frying pan clubs and reached out to grab for the wall, but could not feel it. Panic set in as all of his senses seemed to short circuit.

The Ice Cream Man watched the effects his sensory deprivation liquid was having on Captain Kitchen as he clumsily tried to find some sort of support. The liquid was one of the villain's more ingenious inventions, but the effects were only momentary. If he was going to use the mind control formula, now was the time, and he would have to do it quickly.

He slipped one of the vials containing the formula from his bandolier, and cautiously moved in. This Captain Kitchen had proved himself a worthy opponent, but in the end he too, would fall victim to the formula. Gripping the glass vial tightly, he prepared to make Captain Kitchen his newest pet.

Benji knew he was in real trouble, whatever had been in the vial had completely shut down his senses. It was only a matter of time before the Ice Cream Man attempted to finish him off. He simply could not allow that to happen with so many lives at stake.

The darkness of being blind began to slowly fade, and he could once again see some shadowy shapes. One shape in particular caught his attention, as it seemed to be moving towards him. It had to be the Ice Cream Man moving in for the final strike, so he raised his arm, firing the last projectile from his bracer. With the suddenness of a sonic boom, all of his senses came back, causing a brief sensory overload, dropping him to his knees. As his weight shifted, he jerked his arm upward changing the trajectory of the one time butter knife and nylon rope. The knife connected with the wrist of the Ice Cream Man, which in turn caused the villain to release his grip on the glass vial. It fell from his hand to the concrete floor of the passageway, where it shattered harmlessly.

Finally in control of his senses, Benji climbed to his feet, ready to resume the fight in time to see the damage his knife projectile caused. The Ice Cream Man seemed stunned by his unfortunate luck, then he literally jumped up and down in a rage.

"No! No! No!" the crazed villain screamed, continuing his tantrum.

Benji, still a bit shaken by the sudden wave of sensory information that washed over him, tried to reach out with his hand and grab the incensed villain, but all he managed to grab was a fist full of the Ice Cream Man's coat. The villain quickly spun around, pulling his arms free of the coat, and like a bullet, raced down the corridor. Benji tossed the jacket aside, and hurriedly gave chase.

He could not let the Ice Cream Man get away now. He could hear his nemesis up ahead, catching up in time to see the villain turn a corner. He slowed as he approached the same corner, wary of an ambush. When he heard the telling ding of an elevator, he dashed around just in time to see the Ice Cream Man disappear into an awaiting elevator.

Benji raced to the front of the elevator, but it was too late. The doors had already shut, sealing him out. He scanned the immediate area, but there seemed to be no other means of following. The corridor ended in a dead end a few feet away, and he knew there was no other access from the passage he had just come from. His only option was to wait until the elevator returned.

He located the keypad on the right side, and immediately pushed the button several times, hoping somehow his urgency would be transmitted through his fingertip into the electrical components. Stranger things had happened, including a lunatic calling himself the Ice Cream Man kidnapping the mayor and holding Range City under siege.

After several seconds—which felt like forever—the elevator returned, and the doors slid open. He pushed the up button, and waited to be whisked to who knew where.

When the doors finally opened, he stepped out into yet another tunnel. This one was much shorter in length however, and he could only go straight ahead; at the other end he could plainly see a ladder leading up. The tunnel looked as if it had been converted from a crawl space, and he surmised he must be directly under a dwelling of some sorts.

Sprinting down the tunnel, he reached the ladder within seconds, and did not hesitate to climb up. The ladder went up about ten feet with a trap door covering the exit at the top. The Ice Cream Man could be right on the other side of the door, waiting to catch him off guard with another one of those deadly vials, but it was a chance he would have to take. He had made it this far, he would have to continue to hope his luck would hold out for a little while longer.

Benji paused on the top rung of the ladder, testing the door with his hand, and was not all that surprised to find it was unlocked. After taking a few deep breaths to steel his resolve, he gathered himself and, with as much strength as he could muster, shoved the trap door open. He then pulled himself through the opening as fast as he could.

He found himself standing in a bedroom. He'd wondered why the trap door hadn't made a sound when he hit it so hard, but the 70s gold shag carpet answered that question. It appeared the Ice Cream Man was not only a power hungry whack job, but he had extremely poor taste as well.

A little disorientated from being underground for so long, Benji was comforted by the sight of the sun shining through a window. He knew they had been in the tunnels beneath Range City for several hours, but as least the sun had not set yet. He spotted the bedroom door, and quickly exited. Out in the hallway, he looked around to get his bearings. Off to the left he could see that the hall led to the living room. He was heading there when the banging of a door closing led his focus elsewhere.

The sound had come from the kitchen, which opened off the living room. Once there, he could see the door he assumed had caused the noise. He actually smiled when he saw the Ice Cream Man through the window, walking towards what looked like a garage. "I've got you now Ice Cream Man," he said, heading outside.

In the distance he could hear the faint sound of police sirens. It would seem the chief had gotten through, and figured out where they were at. At one time those sirens would have triggered feelings of frustration as the knowledge of another crime being committed would have hit home. Now, he was elated; the cavalry was coming to the rescue.

He reached into one of his oversized pockets, and pulled out one of his homemade cooking oil grenades. The Ice cream Man was so intent on getting to the garage he had not noticed him yet. He gauged the distance, throwing the grenade with perfect precision, and it landed directly in front of the villain, where it detonated, covering everything within three feet in slippery cooking oil. With the ground now as slippery as ice, the Ice Cream Man slipped, head over heels, doing a complete somersault before landing on his back.

Benji could not help but laugh at the comical scene.

"Alright Ice Cream Man, you've no where left to run. I think it's about time you surrendered."

The evil villain was so incensed by his embarrassing and extremely ungraceful fall, that what little hold he had on his sanity flew right out the proverbial window. After several attempts trying to stand, the Ice Cream Man was finally able to get back to his feet, seething with rage, and the hatred he felt towards Captain Kitchen was almost tangible it was so strong.

"Surrender? You think you have defeated me? Never!" the crazed villain said, answering his own question.

Benji could see in his nemesis's eyes that the light of sanity had clearly burned out. He slowly reached around his back, into his pack and pulled out his newly made whisk bolas. With the plastic blaster out of commission for the time being, the bolas was the only item left he could use to contain the Ice Cream Man from afar.

"As long as I have this," the now irrational Ice Cream Man ranted, spittle flying from his lips as he pulled out the last vial of mind control formula. "You will *never* defeat me."

Benji watched curiously as the villain pulled out the stopper from a glass test tube, and then charged headlong directly at him. His curiosity quickly turned to focused intensity as he pulled forth his whisk bolas, twirled it over his head fiercely, and let it fly.

The reinforced steel whisks and lightweight nylon cord went spinning through the air, closing the distance in seconds. The throwing weapon met the heedless Ice Cream Man head on, wrapping itself around the villain's upper body securely. The villian's arms were tied around his chest, similar to how the Egyptian mummies were often posed.

The Ice Cream Man never knew what hit him. So focused was he on getting to Captain Kitchen and forcing the foolish hero to drink the mind control formula, that he never saw the weapon coming. When the bolas smacked into him, tying his arms to his chest, the wind knocking from him, he was thrown backwards to the ground. He still clutched the glass vial containing the formula in his right hand. To his horror, the liquid formula spilled from the vial onto his mouth and when his lungs finally decided to work again, he inadvertently sucked the mind control formula down his throat, along with a fresh dose of oxygen. He felt the effects take hold immediately, and knew his perfect plan had been foiled.

Benji heard the sharp intake of breath from his fallen adversary. He jogged over only to find the Ice Cream Man lying on the ground, the now familiar dreamy and faraway expression on his evil face.

"The jig is up Ice Cream Man, its time for you to answer for the trouble you've caused."

"Whatever you say Mr. Kitchen," the villain said, his voice somewhat slurred. "I'll do whatever you tell me to."

Benji shook his head out of amusement. Whatever was in that vial must have been some good stuff, and he ventured a guess it would probably explain the strange behavior of the teenagers and Mayor Martinez.

At that moment several police cruisers pulled into the driveway. Range City police officers jumped out with weapons drawn and adrenaline pumping.

"Its OK, stand down."

Upon hearing the voice, Benji turned to look behind him and saw Chief Anderson emerge from the house with the mayor safely in tow.

"You get him?" the chief asked.

"Yeah, I don't think we will be having any more trouble from the Ice Cream Man. At least not for a while anyway," he answered.

CHAPTER 25
The Adventure Begins...

A breeze kicked up, causing the blue apron/cape to flap in the wind. Captain Kitchen stood high atop Range City, on what was fast becoming his regular vantage point—the roof of City Hall. From there he could survey most of the downtown district, and even see the lights of the outlying suburbs. He took in a deep breath of fresh air, and stood proudly watching over his city.

Several weeks had passed since the apprehension of the evil genius, the Ice Cream Man. Range City was slowly returning to normal in the aftermath of the villain's short lived crime spree. Crime in general was on a steady decline, and was currently at an all time low. He felt a great sense of pride knowing the citizens of Range City could sleep a little easier at night.

Within days of the Ice Cream Man's capture, the effects of the formula began to wear off and the teenagers returned to normal. Well, what they considered to be normal, anyway. All the money and stolen property were returned to the rightful owners, and things were right with the world once again.

Mayor Martinez also recovered from his ordeal with the formula with no ill after effects. Though he did have to be sequestered within his private residence for a while, for fear of being persuaded by the City Council into handing out large pay raises and favors.

Once the mind control formula had fully worn off, the mayor gave Chief Anderson a commendation for his actions, and to everyone's surprise held a special ceremony in which he presented Captain Kitchen with the key to the city. It was one of Benji's proudest moments. The outpouring of support and acceptance by the citizens of Range City was overwhelming. It also laid the groundwork for a special relationship that he hoped would last for what would be many years to come.

The Ice Cream Man was held in the Range City Prison. Shortly after the news story broke, several high ranking military officials showed up with extradition papers, claiming the Ice Cream Man was an escaped federal prisoner. He was turned over to the military with no questions asked.

As a former captain in the Army, Benji had to admit he had never seen that division before. He guessed them to be from a branch of military intelligence. If that was true, it would explain why they confiscated everything from the Ice Cream Man's house and secret laboratory. The Ice Cream Man himself had to be dragged from his cell, literally kicking and screaming, by the military officials. Wherever they were taking him, he obviously did not want to go. Before they were able to toss the crazed villain into their waiting van, he swore he would get his revenge against Range City, and Captain Kitchen in particular. Somehow, Benji felt the Ice Cream Man might make good on that threat.

Since that time, things could not have gone any better for him. Captain Kitchen was given complete autonomy by the police, so long as he kept them apprised of information they might need. This was handy, as he no longer needed to skulk around in alleys worrying about being arrested. And, once word of this new partnership spread through the criminal underground, most crooks packed up and moved on to ply their unlawful trades elsewhere. Range City was becoming a safe place to raise a family once again.

His thoughts turned to Jimmy as the breeze picked up once again. It was the young cook's words and untimely passing that had finally stirred him into action. He owed this new life to Jimmy, and felt a sadness knowing he would never get the chance to say thank you. The mourning of his friend soon passed, as his thoughts turned to justice. Every time he captured a crook or thwarted some evil plot, he would be honoring the memory of his dear friend, and in this he took his greatest comfort.

The cell phone he was wearing at his waist began playing the theme from "Superman," causing him to jump. He still had not gotten used to the phone the chief had given him in case the police were ever in need of his services. He reached down, grabbed the phone, and flipped it open.

"Yes, Chief," he answered.

"You ready for some action, Captain Kitchen?" the grizzled voice of Chief Anderson asked from the other end.

"Always."

"Good, because we got a 319 in progress over on Jagers Avenue. Looks like multiple suspects. We might need a hand."

"I'm on my way, Chief."

"We'll see you there."

He clipped the phone back to his waist, and took one last look out over the city before heading to the back of the roof. A special pole had been set up for him to use there, and waiting at the bottom to whisk him to the scene of the crime, was his Harley Sportster. Grabbing the pole and preparing to slide down, he felt the familiar rush of adrenaline kick in. He lived for this. It was time to go to work.

It was hero time.

About the Author

Shawn Oetzel was born and raised in Central Illinois where he still lives with his wife, three kids, and their frustratingly lovable pet pooches, Hemingway and Molly. When not working or writing his next project, Shawn can be found attending his children's many extracurricular activities, or tucked away in his favorite corner at home, losing himself in the pages of another good book.

The Adventrues of Captain Kitchen is Shawn's third novel; his first, *Dying Moon*, was published in 2009 by LBF Books, rereleased by Dark Recesses Press in 2018. His second novel, *The Agency*, was released from Belfire Press in August of 2012 and rereleased by Dark Recesses Press in 2018.

Shawn has always dreamed of being a superhero, knight, or a writer. He is ecstatic he has made good on at least one of those endeavors.